WNWG Presents...

A collection of short stories from the
Wednesday Night Writing Group

Joseph E. Arrowsmith
K. W. Koocher
Anthony Marchionda, Jr.
Lawrence Payne

To our friends and family, for their encouragement and support.

And a special thanks to Arya-Francesca Jenkins for bringing us together and making this book possible.

Forward

By Joseph E. Arrowsmith

When I was a high school student growing up in East Liverpool Ohio, my father showed me this quote from Winston Churchill. The part of this quote that stayed in my mind read, "....it is a riddle wrapped in a mystery cloaked in an enigma."

For twenty-five years, I thought that the old Prime Minister was talking about life in general, but as it turns out, he was talking about the Russians. For my part, I think that Mr. Churchill should have been talking about all of us instead of just one group of people living in just one part of the earth.

I believe this because I see all of life as an unfolding mystery. The magical is mixed in with every aspect of our mundane world. You can see this when you pick up a seashell in your backyard that was left behind when a half billion year old sea -a sea that covered the spot where you now stand- retreated and left this one reminder of itself behind. Think also of faces we see in mountainsides and try to imagine how many myths and campfire stories were inspired by those formations over the last thousand years. Or, if you want to think on a cosmic scale, find an open place and look up into a clear summer night. Certainly some of the stars that you see no longer exist in the physical world. Millions of years before they might have exploded into non-existence, yet the vision of their death has not yet reached our eyes. Hold in your mind the idea that they only exist in the form of an image formed by light. They are only ghosts of their former selves.

Human life too, is often only a mask. Happiness conceals sorrow, and the past lives on in the present. Everyone that you meet on the street is a universe of desires, sorrows and unspoken joys. There are no truly simple lives.

Think about these things as you read our stories and remember to seek out the magic that lies hidden in the fabric of our work-a-day lives. I think you will find that the wonders of our world are all around us.

Table of Contents

Introduction

The Wednesday Night Writing Group members initially met while taking a non-credit fiction writing class at Mahoning County Career & Technical Center. We soon found that we represented an amazingly diverse blend of writing styles and genres. Despite this, or maybe because of it, we managed to form a group that supports and encourages the creative efforts of all members.

After the class officially ended, we continued to meet at our usual time on Wednesday nights. The group began as a way for us to learn more about our craft. It has become much more than that. It has grown into a collection of strong friendships, a forum for our multi-faceted work and a way for us to improve our skills. Despite our many varied writing styles, backgrounds and beliefs we have come to respect each other's differences and to grow, not only as writers but as people too.

The group has enabled us to keep growing as writers and has nurtured the bonds of friendship and trust that started during that long ago writer's course. Before the creation of the group, we could only share our writings with our friends and families. Now, we have the knowledge, the confidence and the skills to share our work with the world.

We invite you to read our works.

Joseph E. Arrowsmith

Joseph E. Arrowsmith was born in East Liverpool Ohio and is a life long resident of the Buckeye State.

He is a reader, a writer, and a Respiratory Therapist. Currently, he lives in Campbell, Ohio with his wife, Mirta, his two children Matthew and Samantha, and a good poodle named Dan.

Leo's Gift

Joseph E. Arrowsmith

Thomas Caine broke camp at sundown and rode out onto open grasslands. In his saddlebags he carried a map, a compass, and some light provisions. What he left behind were the carbon remains of Julia's letters that still smoked in the embers of his fire.

For a long while after sunset, he rode toward Polaris, following the natural swell of the land. A full Hunter's Moon lit his way and cast a pale light on the prairie sea.

Around midnight he stopped on a bluff and took out his binoculars. Scanning slowly to the north, he saw the first "man pillar" that marked the southern boundaries of the Tribal Lands. He thought for a moment that he might be mistaken, but then he saw the Great Crow perched on the brave's broad shoulder.

"Almost there," he said as he nudged his horse into a gentle trot.

By one A.M. he had reached the first "man". Up close the giant figure became only a tall stack of polished river stones. Its human qualities were a product of distance, light, and shadow. Even the crow, perched on the brave's shoulder, disintegrated into a jagged amalgamation of quartz and slate. Under the crow's wing he stopped and gazed down at the note that his father had written on the map two decades ago. It read, *One Guardian every quarter mile until river. Stop at third.*

Tom rode over the waves of the solid sea as he followed the Guardians. Twenty years ago, when he had been a boy of eight tethered to his granddad's saddle horn, the up and down motion had made him laugh. Back then Gramps rode point in front of Tommy and his pony. Dad, for his part, held back to "Watch out for them Kansas ky-yotes."

Now, the two men who had raised him were 18 years dead, and he was alone. Just as he was meant to be.

"It's just how it turned out," he had told Julia just three days before at the dance. "The fire. The years in the Wichita Boy's home. It's all taught me that I'm meant to be alone."

Julia touched him gently on the cheek and said, "I will send you a sign. Come home to me, Thomas Caine."

On the way out of the brightly lit barn, Dr. Colwell had stopped him and said, "Remember son, signs are sometimes like the Guardians. A lot depends on your point of view."

All these memories, both near and distant, receded from his mind as he approached the next stone sentinel. Now he had to be careful not to...

The front hoof of his horse came down on the rock and he knew he was there. Dismounting, he guided his horse a step back. There, under the outline of a hoof print, were the names: **EDWARD, ARNOLD, and THOMAS CAINE '68.** Beside the names in a much smaller hand, there was a trace of his own carving that read, Leo lites.

All this time and it was still there. It wasn't overgrown or erased. Some might say that it was a minor miracle in itself... if you believed in such things.

With a smile, Tom spread a blanket across the stone and stretched out on his back. Without looking, he knew that it must be two A.M. It wouldn't be long now.

At that moment, a streak of light passed over his

head. It was fast. It was bright. It was beautiful. Instantly, he was eight years old again.

"You're seeing the Leonid meteor storm, Tommy," Grandpa explained. "When I was your age back in '33, there were even more. The sky was just filled with falling stars.

See, the meteors seem to erupt from Leo's mouth."

"The lion is roaring stars, Daddy!" Tommy had said to his father who was trying to settle his son's nervous pony.

"Yes, son," his father had said. "That's something that your mother would have said..." Here, Arnold Caine's voice trailed off before he continued, "You just remember this birthday, Tommy, and keep your heart open to the wonders of the world."

The grown up Caine tried to count the streaks, but soon there were too many. More and more came until hundreds of falling stars filled the whole dome of the night sky.

"This is what grandpa saw when he was a boy," Tom said to his horse which looked down on him. "You could live 10 lifetimes and never see this."

In his mind, he could see Julia's face. That all-knowing look was in her eye.

"It's going to take more than that," he said.

Then, suddenly, it happened.

A searing ball of flame, about the size of a peach basket, shot just past the shoulder of the next Guardian to the north. The rush of sound -a high pitched whistling whine- caught up later and sent a shock wave through the air.

Caine sprang to his feet and grabbed onto the reins.

With one hand he steadied the horse, while, with the other, he focused his binoculars on the stone Guardian, about an eighth of a mile away.

Under the bright glow of what the Kickapoos called, 'The Buffalo Moon,' Tom saw that the crow, and a portion of the figure's shoulder, had been knocked into the grass.

How many people in human history have ever witnessed a meteor impact? He knew that there could not be many.

Again, Julia's image and words appeared to him and again he pushed them down. "Not yet," he told her, as she faded from his mind.

Caine mounted his horse and trained his binoculars along the seared line of grass leading out from the Guardian's shoulder. It took him time, and he knew that he was unlikely to see anything, yet still he tried. He was just about to give up, when he saw it.

A tree -one of the rare trees that you could see out here -was on fire. It was rooted near the peak of a grassy hill, and it was blazing away.

Tom kicked his horse into a full gallop and set out toward the burning tree. As he rode, he thought of Julia and her hours of scripture reading that had taken up a good part of their courting time. If she were here, she would be quoting to him the passage about God, Moses, and the burning bush.

"I take your point," he said to the chill night air.

When he finally reached the tree, he found that the whole hillside was now in flames. At first, common sense held him back. Then, his boyhood memory of waking up to find his cabin on fire filled his brain. He knew that there was no possible way for him to stand aside and watch *anything* burn.

Cain went to war. He drew his shovel from his pack and, with his kerchief pulled up over his face, waded into the smoke and fire. He shoveled and stomped while the smoke attacked his eyes and the flying cinders singed his clothes. Finally, there was only one more burning patch at the base of the tree to smother.

Caine approached this last remnant of fire just as the sun was rising behind him.

With a feeling of triumph coursing through his veins, he struck this last bit of flames a conqueror's blow… and snapped off the scoop of his shovel on something hard that lay under the burning tree branch. Then he stepped back and looked at what he had done.

It was simple, really. The last blow of his shovel had cleaved the meteor in two.

He guessed that diamond cutters did this all the time on purpose. He, on the other hand, had done the same thing by accident.

It was about the size of a turkey egg. The inside of the stone was cut clean and showed the tell tale wicker pattern of an authentic meteorite, just like in Grandpa's book. Caine saw that some of this "wicker" contained black, gray, and golden flecks of minerals all scattered around the core in a random pattern.

Or was it random?

Caine stood up and walked around the stone, a gift

from the constellation Leo, and saw it.

There, just as plain as day --well, he had to tilt the stone up a bit and crouch down on his knees -- was the profile of a woman looking back at him.

It was the woman who loved him. The woman who offered him a true life.

Later, when the stone was cool enough to pack away, he wrapped it in his blanket and tied it to his saddle bag. He figured that Homily was about a four-day ride from here.

That would be all right. With a bit of good luck, he would arrive on Julia's birthday with a very special gift.

The Rift

Joseph E. Arrowsmith

He bore the weight of his many years on his back as he hobbled to the rift that yawned open before him. Already he had passed the monuments capped by brass helmets that rested on bronze picks and shovels. There, at the six graves, he had paused to recall the words of his grandmother, who in his youth had told him, *"Hell is a real place, boy,"* He could see her boney finger in motion even now. *"It lies at the end of a wicked road and is fashioned by the damned one's own hands."*

Earlier, back in the city, he had told a priest in the confessional about what his Grandma Pearl had said and what he intended to do. The young Father had listened and then tried to reason with his parishioner, but nothing he said could change the older man's mind.

On that day, Henry left for the Appalachian town of his birth. He had not been home for many decades, so great was his shame. He passed briefly through the main street of this small place and then drove up into the remote mountainside that held the graves and, beyond them, the rift.

Leaving the markers behind, he labored to reach the dark slit that opened in the hillside. As he climbed, he recalled the last words of his crew leader. *"Go Little Henry,"* Big Jake had said after the cave in. *"Crawl through that narrow space and feed me back that timber so that I can shore up the ceiling. Then go for help and bring back a rescue team."*

Henry had then crawled through the narrow gap quickly enough, but once on the other side, he simply ran away without making any attempt to pass back the beam. In a sheer panic he pursued a lost course that took him nowhere, and when he finally did reach help, there were none left alive to report his shame.

Now Henry paused as he stood before the black slit that cut down the side of the mountain. In preparation for this journey he carried only a box of biscuits and a gallon of water wrapped in his old green army blanket. He planned to walk into this abandoned shaft on a penitential march that would take him deep within the mountain. For light he carried with him only a single stub of candle that was no longer than his thumb. Its length and light would have to suffice for the time of his stay in this place.

With a steady pace, Henry entered the mine. Soon all daylight vanished and he was left in darkness so complete that it weighed down upon him like a soaking blanket.

Lighting the candle with one of only a dozen matches, he said the name of the first miner. He then marched forward one pace for each year that had passed between the time of the cave-in and now before he again extinguished the flame and dropped to the ground. "There," he told some sightless creature that ran across his knees, "This is the hell that awaits Ol' Henry at the end of his days."

Time passed in this way until Henry reached the third name of *Jacob Cummings*. This name he called out at the top of his lungs. Its sound echoed through the silent tunnels. This time, however, a deep masculine voice responded saying, "I have come for you Henry Talbot. Stay where you are."

Henry would have run, but his legs were frozen to the tunnel floor. He could do nothing but wait until a lanterned helmet appeared from behind a beam. Under the light was a giant of a man with a red beard who said, "I've come to take you away from here."

"Jake!" Henry said recognizing the face in the candle light. "You've come from heaven and I am in hell. Go back and leave me to my fate."

The big man replied." I am Jacob's grandson and, in his honor, I carry his name."

At this, the living Jacob Cummings sat down beside Henry and said, "Here, I have something to show you before we leave this place."

As the big man unwrapped a small bundle, Henry asked, "how did you find me?"

"Your priest broke his vows and called our home this morning. He gave us every particular of your plans so it was not hard to find you."

Jacob hushed Henry before he could speak again and then pushed a little piece of paper that was pressed between two squares of glass into the old man's hand. "Read this," he said. "When we went back down to the site of the accident six months ago, I found this inside a buried canteen. It's from my grandfather."

Henry focused his eyes and read: ***All of us forgive Henry. He is just nineteen and a good boy to his kin. - J. Cummings***

After they had read the note several times, young Jake stood Henry on his feet and wrapped his great hand around the old man's shoulder. "Come on now Mr. Talbot. They're making dumplings down at the church social. Everyone knows you're here and everyone is waiting."

"But I don't deserve…'

"Who among us deserves anything, Mr. Talbot?" Jake said as they walked toward the day. "But then, that's what God is for."

No more was said until they emerged from the tunnel. There, they were met by a dozen arms that escorted them toward the light of Good Hope, Kentucky. The group of Henry's friends and their children guided the old man back down the treacherous path. They did not hurry, but they did not pause. When Henry stumbled on a patch of ice, Jacob's brother caught him and stood him upright again. In this way they made steady progress and, in good time, they left the darkness of the rift far behind them.

Section 19

Joseph E. Arrowsmith

I Ride

I ride the train between Sedgewick and Oxford. I ride everyday because that's who I am. I sit in the rear seat with my pad and my pencil and sketch people and objects that I spy from the train.

Some call me "The Pass Man Who Rides All of the Day" between the two stops of Sedgewick and Oxford.

I ride with Headmasters escorting day school excursions, and men with thin shoes that come to a point. When the *Four* rolls in, I am given wide birth to take my far seat across from the door.

Where I crouch and do sketches of the places I pass. My favorite's a graveyard that rests on a hill and holds granite statues with wide-open wings. One Angel I see — why something has changed— has shoes tied by long laces that drape over his wings.

I leap up excited and point out the window, but all my companions cast down their dull eyes. Still one in the front, who is a Writer/Reporter, makes a note on his pad then returns to his work.

Leaving me standing and rocking in silence as the Oxford Express rolls past Section 19.

I Stand

I stand near the angels on Homily Hill, sipping tea from a thermos in Section 19. I come every day when the north gate swings open---the gates south of Sedgewick, not far from tracks. On my shoulder I carry a sack with good paper, plus charcoal, and film for my pocket Kodak.

I sketch lambs and cherubs and wheat bundles on stone. The symbol of a very long life I am told. I rub till the chalk breaks over a dove at the feet of the grandest angel I've seen.

I call him Gabriel and he speaks to my heart as he looks down on the children of 1918. "The Sad year of the Flu" says a prayer on a plaque read out by Bob Daniels eight decades ago.

My heart calls me to action so I take off my shoes. Then I knot up the laces and throw them over the wings. Now someone will notice, if just for an instant, the boys lying buried in Section 19.

The Boys

The Boys came from Shelby, Sedgewick and Oxford and all lived at the school in 1918. The Train Writer/Reporter asks," How many were there?" and Old Bob replies, "There were one short of twenty," as he points to the plot near the tracks of the train.

Where an Angel's wide wings hold a silent indictment of the ancient Headmaster peering down through the rain.

Bob says, "See these bronze shoes hung with link chain behind me? I've kept each pair attached there since 1918."

"Will, Tom, Dave, and Dennis," the Writers picks names from a pad on his lap. "They died with the others of the "Flu From the Trenches" "The Spanish Catastrophe," the papers all read.

Old Bob, the Headmaster, leans over and says, "All died with dark secrets asleep in their beds. In that terrible year when our soldiers brought with them a sickness from France, those secrets were leaking; what else could I do?"

"The Truth," said the Writer.

"Ah, that's easy for you.

Instead I brought blankets from the Sick Soldiers Pavilion and tucked the boys in on those chill autumn nights. And after they passed--- it was all over by snowfall--- and the boys rested sound under Homily Hill…"

"You burned the green blankets one night in the furnace and said prayers by the graves with a heart full of ill."

"Yes, it was all long ago, but see now the Angel? The shoes hang by string cast over the wing. Done by someone who knows what I've done, I'm sure. Of the sins that I buried in 1918. Near the tracks where the FOUR runs from Sedgewick to Oxford, past the stone shoe-winged Gabriel of Section 19."

Chimes

Its twenty months later and old Bob is now ashes. He was picked up by the current and released from his cell. While on Homily Hill, old Gabe does his duty standing guard with bronze shoes attached to his wings.

Each shoe, suspended, chimes in with the others, when a breeze stirs the graveyard by the side of the trains.

In summer comes the Artist, the Writer and Rider and all place a red rose in the links of the chains. They pray and the third asks, "Those bronze shoes..., how many? Is there two for each child 'cause that's how it seems?"

The Grave Artist answers, "Yes there's one short of twenty. Each pair fits a boy in Section 19."

The Prize

Joseph E. Arrowsmith

They dropped him so far down into the crater that he lost the light entirely. "This had better be worth it," Henry said as his boots came to rest on a narrow outcrop of stone.

There he paused to collect his nerve while several rocks, kicked loose by his landing, fell away into the blackness below.

Henry took a deep breath, collected himself, and swept the beam of his miner's helmet to the left until he found the crack in the wall. Then, after dialing down the light to its lowest setting, he carefully unsnapped the clippers from his belt and peered into the deep gash that the meteor had cut on some unknown and ancient day.

Right away, he saw something inside. It was clear, reflective, and animated. "You can't run," Henry called into the little black hole. "Nothing will stop me from winning the prize." At this, Henry plunged both his free right hand and his left that held the clipper into the opening.

Five minutes later and the struggle was over. Exhausted but triumphant -and minus the titanium clippers that had been given to him by his garden club-Henry gave the signal to the men waiting above.

As the winch pulled him upward, his heart filled with joy and pride. Never in his life had he ever won anything of any significance. He imagined the speeches, the applause, and the attention of the media.

All of these imaginings lasted until he reached the sunlight. That was when the only living crystal rose in existence gave a tiny shriek and dissolved in his hand. Its dead remains, shining like ground diamonds in the sunlight, slipped through Henry's fingers and drifted back into the darkness waiting below.

Taps

Joseph E. Arrowsmith

Under the wings of an angel, at the crest of Homily Hill, a young boy plays taps over three graves. The first two graves are settled and marked with his first and last name. The third, however, bears the name of a stranger and is still free from the prairie grass that will stake its claim in the spring.

In this newest grave are the bones of a long lost soldier. He was found only a few months ago when French workers broke ground for a new roadside rest. It was on the third scoop of the excavator when the remains of Albert Henry Wallace returned to the sunlight.

The ten-year-old boy, whose name is Mitchell Harding III, doesn't know anything about the old bones at his feet. All he cares about is pleasing his grandmother who stands beside him in a mink stole and white gloves. "They were clothes from my young days Little Mitch," she had told him this morning.

Soon, however, the last note of Taps fades away and Little Mitch asks, "Can we get some hot chocolate now grandma?"

"In a few minutes dear," Augustina says. "Play something Big Band for me, please?"

Mitchell, who would have played with blue lips for an attentive audience of penguins, put his discomfort aside and started in with *This Joint's a Jumpin'*.

Augustina Harding tilted her head and closed her eyes. Immediately she lost herself in the memory of a happy week spent with an army musician from Lawrence.

They had met here on Homily Hill while her own husband was a patient in a military psychiatric unit in the Pacific theater.

She had been tending flowers on a warm May morning with the letter from her husband's doctors stuffed deep in the pocket of her apron .The letter contained the phrases *'intractable shell shock'*, and *'long term care'* in its contents. It was then that she heard someone playing a muted trumpet behind her.

Augustina turned just as the young man came up behind her and said, "Oh excuse me Miss. I'm sorry if I've disturbed you. I was just playing a bit over my grandmother's grave. We were always close you see…"

It was here that he smiled. From that point on she didn't hear the rest of his words.

The next week passed in a blur of fire and passion. She left town for seven days and told no one where she had gone. On Sunday morning, the day after Albert shipped out for England, the sheriff arrived on her doorstep just hours after she had returned home. In his hand he carried a telegram saying that her husband would be arriving by train in Homily early Monday morning and that he would be accompanied by a volunteer from the Mental Service Corp.

A wave of guilt washed over her and threatened to drown her spirit. The wave crested when a white and speechless Mitchell stepped down from the train supported by the arm of his escort.

That night she cried while her husband stared up at the empty ceiling. It was the first of countless nights without love, affection, or even recognition. During these early days guilt transformed itself into a dark and heavy despair that hung around her neck like a yoke.

Then, in the third month, as she was scrubbing out

her husband's soiled underwear in a laundry tub, she noticed that her apron felt tight around her middle. It was in that moment, with her hands covered in rubber gloves and stinking brown water floating before her eyes, that hope returned to heart.

From then on everything was bearable. The nights were as loveless as ever and the days were filled with endless chores and therapy sessions. Once a month there the long drive into Topeka for her husband's evaluation.

It was on one of these trips that Mitchell Jr. was born. He was a large dark haired baby who looked nothing like either of his parents. Over the years when people would rudely comment on his appearance, Augustina would simply say, "Well, it was just God's plan."

When Mitch Jr. was one year old, his true father disappeared in France. When he was a young teen, the man who stared out the window all day long passed away during one of his long afternoon naps. Later he told his mother, "I didn't notice right away. He looked just the same."

Decades passed and Augustina's son married later in life, moved out to the west coast, and then died in a car crash along with his wife. Their new baby, who her son described as "always singing, blowing or bashing something," was home with the sitter at the time.

During all of these years, Augustina wrote twice a year to Albert's family in Lawrence. Each time she asked if he had been found. Always, the answer was no.

Then one day ten years after she received custody of Mitchell Harding III, she came across an article in a news magazine. It was just sitting there open in the waiting room of her dentist's office right beside her chair. The headline read: **BODIES OF SIX MIA's FOUND IN FRANCE.**

Augustina never got her tooth filled on that day. She might have gone ahead if Albert's name hadn't been listed three down from the top. But, as it was, she walked out without answering to the receptionist who followed her out onto the sidewalk.

All that day she stayed at home and made phone calls. Through the letters that she kept from Albert's family in Lawrence she tracked down Albert's last remote relative who was some third cousin used car dealer out in Fresno California. A thousand dollars sent by Western Union was all it took to allow Albert's remains to be shipped back to Homily Hill Cemetery.

It was a place where a seventy-year-old woman and her ten-year-old grandson could come and visit on a bitter winter afternoon. Here she could come and remember Albert and the one-week they had spent together that had transformed her life.

Augustina looked down at the boy who had just finished his tune and asked, *Will I ever tell him? No, she answered herself. What would be the point?*

Down at her side, little Mitchell Harding the Third touched his grandma on the sleeve and asked. "Can I play one more before we go?"

Augustina's eyes filled with tears as she remembered Albert's question on the morning before they left the cemetery on that day over fifty years ago. He was dressed in his uniform and stood before her with his trumpet in his hands. He asked, "Can I play one you'd like to hear?"

For one moment that lasted as long as a dozen heart beats, Augustina stood with her feet in two worlds. Her young self spoke to the handsome man in uniform, while her older self spoke to a waist high boy who played the trumpet like his granddad.

To both she said, "Please play *Begin the Beguine*. I've always liked that one."

At once, both in her memory and in reality, the melody drifted over the stones of Homily Hill and lifted her heart. To the young woman so long ago, it brought the promise of escape and selfish pleasure.

To the old woman, who stood beside her grandson with her hand touching his shoulder, the music filled her mind with peace and drove the last vestige of guilt from her soul.

When the music had stopped, Augustina kissed Mitch on the cheek and repeated the same lines that she spoke fifty years ago. "Come on," she said "You and I have places to go."

With this said, both the dream man, made only of memory, and the ten year old made from flesh and bone, tucked their instrument under their arms, took the hand of Augustina Harding and walked away from the graves on Homily Hill.

K. W. Koocher

K. W. Koocher was born in Pittsburgh, Pennsylvania. A wanderer in her youth, she spent several years touring the country on foot and by thumb.

She is a 1991 graduate of LaGuardia College in New York City and worked as the veterinary technician at the Queens Zoo for many years.

She currently lives in Youngstown, Ohio with long-suffering husband Mike and an ever-increasing brood of rescued alley cats.

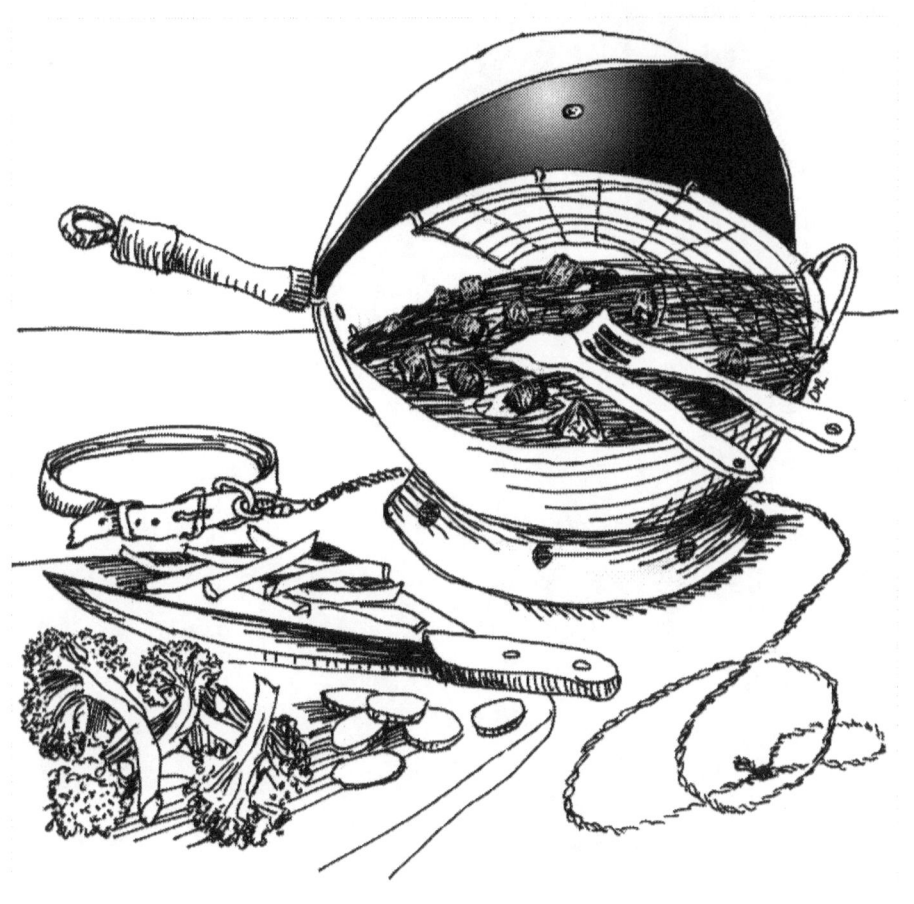

Dr. Carver's Delicious Stir Fry

K. W. Koocher

Dr. Carver sighed as he turned away from the table. It had been a long surgery, and for a while there he had almost thought Fido Smith would have many more years of crapping on the carpet and gnawing on the furniture in his doggy future. After nearly two hours of his best efforts, though, the Great Dane's heart had finally signaled "Game Over".

"Death by Rubber Ball," his technician Jenny grumbled as she stared disconsolately down at the steel kick bucket. The once gleaming and pristine vessel now contained nearly a gallon of bloody saline, in which floated several feet of Fido's small intestine and the offending rubber ball.

Fido had swallowed the ball approximately two weeks ago, and his owners had waited until rigor mortis was the only symptom of illness the dog hadn't developed before finally breaking down and bringing the mutt to a vet. There had been precious little intestine left in Fido's belly that hadn't degenerated into a blackened, necrotic mess.

The moment he had opened the dog up, Dr. Carver had realized that Fido would only survive with the aid of divine intervention. Still he had tried, hoping for that miracle.

Jenny left the room, returning with a large body bag. Pulling the bag over Fido's head, she struggled to wrap the dog's carcass, prior to taking it downstairs to the basement freezer. As Jenny was all of five feet nothing and weighed considerably less than Fido, this looked to be a bit of a losing battle.

"Jen," Dr. Carver said, laying a gentle hand on her

shoulder, "Eight p.m. has come and gone. You head on home and I'll finish up here."

After a token protest Jenny allowed Dr. Carver to smilingly shoo her out the door. After she departed, he put on a pair of gloves and, taking a scalpel, carefully cut out pieces from several sections of Fido's intestine, most from the necrotic area and a couple from the small amount of healthy tissue that still remained. These he dropped into small jars of formaldehyde and labeled.

Turning the body over, he efficiently peeled the skin away from Fido's hindquarters, then cut away the two large muscle masses that formed the dogs haunches. These he dropped into a large freezer bag, which he sealed tightly and tossed into his briefcase. The formaldehyde jars he left lined up on the counter for Jenny to send out to the lab in the morning.

Afterwards, he finished bagging Fido's carcass and the contents of the kick bucket and bundled them down to the basement freezer. Then he went into his office to call Fido's owner and break the bad news.

That done, he opened his briefcase again, fishing for his address book. He opened the book, running his finger down a page, then picked up the phone and dialed.

"Hello, Sarah, it's Joe Carver," he said into the phone. "How would you like to come over for a late supper tonight?"

He glanced at the freezer bag in his briefcase.

"I'm making stir fry."

The Dreadful Death of
Cousin Arthur

K. W. Koocher

My cousin Arthur died in 1963, the year I turned 21. Arthur was three years older than me, a bespectacled, bookish sort of fellow with severely cropped brown hair and glasses that he was constantly pushing back up the bridge of his long nose. I, like a great many young men at the time, wore my hair very long and tended towards blue jeans and tie dyed t-shirts decorated with anti-war slogans. Arthur, by contrast, was Mr. Suit-and-Tie, his shoes always polished to a dazzling sheen and his tie and handkerchief carefully chosen to match whatever white or pastel starched and pressed button-down shirt he happened to be wearing. Rumor had it that Arthur even ironed his socks.

The greatest passion Arthur ever exhibited was for Pepsi Cola. He adored Pepsi Cola with a devotion that bordered on idolatry. Whenever Arthur had to attend a social function, he did so with several bottles of the stuff stashed surreptitiously about his person, so as not to be at the mercy of whatever brand his hosts might have chosen to buy. As small children, his sisters and I delighted in finding and absconding with his Pepsi whenever we could, leaving poor Arthur to stand thirstily for the remainder of the gathering, as he would not soil his palate with any lesser libation.

To my Aunt Minerva's great pride, her son Arthur was the first of our generation to attend and graduate from college. After he graduated, Arthur enrolled in graduate school, avidly pursuing his Master's Degree in Anthropology. Unlike most young men of the day - who attended graduate school to escape a senior trip to Southeast Asia - Arthur viewed Anthropology with a reverence he had hitherto reserved only for his Pepsi Cola.

Although he looked and acted remarkably like an accountant, Arthur's chosen field of study involved what Aunt Minerva liked to refer to as the "Lost Tribes of Darkest Africa".

During his final year of graduate school, Arthur made numerous journeys to Africa to complete first-hand studies of many of these tribes, their cultures and their customs. It was during one of these trips that Arthur and three of his traveling companions met their fate at the hands of an obscure tribe of cannibals who inhabited a hitherto unexplored swath of jungle deep in the Congo.

We would have never learned of Arthur's fate, except that the fifth member of their expedition, a serious-faced young woman named Delilah Smith, was escorted from the jungle several weeks later by a traveling missionary party after they had discovered her wandering alone outside of the cannibalistic tribe's territory. She was dazed and suffering from fever and insect bites, but in remarkably good condition considering her recent ordeal. She carried a small cloth bag, and otherwise possessed only the ragged remnants of the clothing she had been wearing when the group was surprised by the cannibals. The bag, which she clutched with a convulsive grip, contained all that remained of her deceased colleagues.

Aunt Minerva was notified of Arthur's death by representatives of Uncle Sam, who had in turn been contacted by the American Embassy office in that region of Africa. She promptly called her sister Athena, my mother, and then collapsed in hysterics.

The day that Delilah Smith was due to arrive in the United States, escorting the remains of Arthur and company, Aunt Minerva was still indisposed. Since my mother could not leave her side I was chosen to meet Miss Smith at the airport and take custody of Arthur's body.

When Miss Smith finally cleared customs, she was shown to the small room where I, along with the parents of Arthur's assistant, Richard, anxiously awaited her. With murmured condolences, she rummaged in her luggage, finally producing two small boxes, one for me and one for Richard's parents.

As a mere cousin, she left me until last, spending time with Richard's mother and father first. Finally, after they had murmured their last thanks and shed more tears, the bereaved parents shuffled out, clutching their small box.

When Miss Smith handed me the box containing Arthur's remains, I did something that Richard's parents had not done. I split the tape with a thumbnail and opened it, ignoring her horrified gasp. As I looked into the container, my own shocked inhalation rivaled hers. Instead of ashes, as I had expected, I was looking at a shriveled and mummified human penis.

I slammed the box shut, gawking at the blushing Miss Smith.

"I don't understand this," I spluttered. "However can this be all that is left of Arthur?"

"I can tell you of what befell Arthur and the others, if you've the stomach for it," she replied. Her voice was as crisp and serious-looking as her face, with an accent varying between upper class British and moneyed New England. When I nodded assent, she seated herself at the small table in the center of the room, gesturing me towards the chair opposite hers. Conspicuous young rebel that I was at that time, I turned my chair so that the back faced the table, then straddled it, resting my elbows on the chair back after placing the box containing what was left of Arthur on the table between us. Miss Smith waited until I had arranged myself, then she began her story:

"We had contracted for a guide in the last trading town along the Congo River and, after we finished outfitting ourselves, we set out for the deep jungle. Arthur, who was heading up the expedition, had heard rumors of a tribe that was supposedly located far back in the jungle along an unexplored tributary of the Congo River. This tribe, it was said, had never before been seen by any white man. Our party consisted of myself, Arthur, Richard, who was Arthur's assistant from the university, our guide Tomas, and a local bearer with an unpronounceable African name whom everybody called Joe.

"Tomas proved to be a good and trustworthy guide. We motored up the Congo in a small flatboat, finding the hidden tributary and proceeding along it until it became impassable for the boat. There we concealed the craft in some thick brush and continued the trek on foot. Joe carried most of the foodstuffs and photographic equipment, while the rest of us carried our personal necessities, notebooks and specimen jars. Arthur, of course, also carried two large bottles of Pepsi Cola, which he carefully rationed for himself and about which we all teased him mercilessly.

"The expedition was going very well, and we were all making numerous notes and rapidly filling our specimen jars. Then one morning, midway through the second week of our trek, we stepped into a small clearing

48

to find ourselves surrounded on all sides by nearly naked tribesmen of a type we had never encountered before. They had paint daubed across their faces and bodies, and their spears and arrows looked very sharp and menacing. Unlike other natives we had encountered, none of these men were smiling, or indeed making any effort at communication.

"They relieved us of our machetes and Tomas's gun, then marched us forcibly through the jungle for almost half a day before we came to their village. Once we were there, I was separated from the others and turned over to a group of women, all of whom were busy with different domestic tasks. I was given a crude clay jug, and made to fetch water with two tribes women who appeared to be about my age. We brought the water back from the river and poured it into a great stone pot that occupied the center of the village. It took a couple of hours, and many trips, before we'd finally brought back enough water to satisfy the unfriendly and ancient crone who was directing the proceedings.

"Once there was enough water in the cauldron, a fire was lighted beneath it and two of the older women were assigned to keep the fire burning. As night fell, torches were lit, so many of them that the clearing was as bright as day. Finally, except for the two women feeding the fire, all of the rest of the women gathered in a loose semi circle on the outer rim of the boundary defined by the flickering torches. Four or five men walked slowly into the clearing, beating out a complex rhythm on long narrow drums that hung on thongs from their necks.

"Then a large group of men entered, all of them decorated in bright splashes of paint and wearing jewelry made of shells, stones, bones and feathers. They were singing, their discordant voices somehow blending with the music of the drums. Between them, slung from poles, they carried Arthur, Richard, Tomas and Joe. I bit my lips, somehow stopping myself from crying out. All four had been stripped naked and were already dead.

"The bodies were arranged side by side on the ground by the huge pot. One by one, their murderers used sharp knives and cut away the top half of each body, stopping at their," and here Miss Smith paused a second, blushing to the roots of her short, sensible hair.

"Um, stopping at their, um, thing," she finally said, gesturing towards the box on the table between us. "They then picked up the portions they had cut off and threw them into the pot. These they cooked for awhile, as they continued to play their drums and dance about in the torch light. Then each of the men took a bowl and helped himself to a large portion of stew, and I saw to my sorrow that they washed their grisly feast down with shares of one of Arthur's bottles of Pepsi.

"They covered the remaining portion of the bodies with leaves, and the next night there was a second feast. The drums and dancing were the same, except that this time they cooked the lower half of each body, cutting away and throwing into the pots everything below the men's... um..." She blushed again, then plunged ahead, "Below the men's things."

"They washed this second feast down with shares of Arthur's second bottle of Pepsi. Afterwards, one of the women gathered up my poor companions," another blush, "Um, things, which she took to the edge of the village and buried. That night I crept out of the women's tent, dug up all that remained of my friends and took them with me as I made my escape from the village. They weren't guarding me, and I don't think they even bothered to pursue me. It struck me as a rather chauvinistic society." She said this with an audible sniff.

There was a long silence following her narrative, then I shook my head. "I don't get it, " I said. "These cannibals ate their bones, their internal organs, even their hair. Why wouldn't they eat their, um, their things?" This last I said lamely, blushing myself as I glanced at Miss Smith.

Miss Smith stared at me as if I had gone quite mad. "The savages," she sniffed, "Had only Arthur's Pepsi with which to wash down their repast."

My bafflement must have shown in my face, because her expression softened somewhat as she explained.

"Young man," she said, not unkindly. "Things go better with Coke."

Charlie's End

K. W. Koocher

"Yes, but...", Sheila began. This was her sixth "yes, but..." in as many minutes. Carrie could feel her irritation cycle up a notch and mentally thumbed her self control button.

"There are no buts here, Sheila," Joe's voice was soft, his tone patient. Joe was always patient, even in a situation like this one. Carrie could find patience only for the children and couldn't fathom how Joe could always maintain his inner calm, whatever the level of idiocy he found himself having to deal with.

Carrie herself would have explained the situation by connecting her size six shoe directly with Sheila's size 18 derriere. All things considered, Joe's method of handling these emotionally charged situations was probably better than hers would have been. Which is why everybody at Ramon had no trouble snapping to when he opened his mouth, whether it was a request to pass the salt at dinner or more ammo during a firefight. One of the myths circulating about Joe held that he'd once mumbled 'fire' in his sleep and six troopers blew away an unsuspecting maple tree while a seventh started a blaze in the middle of the parade ground.

"I understand what you're feeling," Joe continued. His voice was soft and his expression was one of genuine regret. He focused on Sheila as he spoke, ignoring Carrie at his elbow and the harsh sounds drifting in through the back door, which was standing ajar. "I really do, and God knows I wish we could make an exception. The fact is, though, that you're endangering everybody here. We don't have a lot of rules, but this one is written in stone. I'm sorry. I really am. But it has got to be put down."

Sheila glanced towards the open door connecting

the small kitchen in which they stood to the long back yard. It wasn't much of a yard, just a patch of dying crabgrass fronting a dozen concrete-floored dog runs, the chain link walls forming them rising to almost eight feet in height. The runs were covered by wood and shingle roofing to protect the inhabitants from the elements. Before the end of the world, as in five months ago, the twelve canine army members assigned to Fort Ramon had occupied these runs.

There was no reason to confine the army dogs, or any of the animals that had been retrieved from local homes and apartments, because none of the animals ever attempted to leave Ramon. The soldiers made their rescue attempts in hope of finding stranded humans, but none of the squad members ever complained about rescuing a dog or cat. Or parrot, bunny, hamster or iguana. Any life saved was a mark in the plus column as far as the inhabitants of Ramon were concerned.

Carrie followed Sheila's glance. She was standing behind Joe and could only see a small patch of grass and a bit of fence through the back door. She didn't need to see the runs to know what was housed there, though. The rattling of chain link and the growling of the current occupant were constant, never pausing for rest or to take a breath. The sound wafting through the door grated on Carrie's nerves, although she had almost ceased hearing the much louder version that constantly beat against Ramon's walls.

"But he's locked up!" Sheila protested. "The run is padlocked. Nobody can get in, and he can't get out. Nothing will happen, I promise! I swear on my mothers life!"

56

"Oh, for shits sake!" Carrie was out of patience. "You're acting like a kid with a stray dog. It isn't a God damned dog. You don't have Spot or Fido in there, you have a fucking zombie. You can't keep a fucking zombie for a pet, Sheila. Next you'll want to teach it tricks and take it for a walk down Main Street. Quit being such a fucking moron!"

"He's not a zombie, Carrie!" Sheila snapped, her voice losing its usual Brooklyn accent for a moment in angry mimicry of Carrie's Uptown inflections. "That's my Charlie and he's not one of them! He's hurt bad but he's not dead and don't you go telling people he is! He's just sick! Charlie isn't dead!"

Joe raised a hand as Carrie opened her mouth to retort. "No, Sheila," he said, his tone still gentle. "It WAS Charlie, and he is dead. What you have back there is a monster wearing his body. Your Charlie is dead and now it's up to you to do the right thing here. If there's anything left of Charlie in there, do you honestly think he'd want this? To be locked in a dog run to decay nice and slow while he bangs himself silly on the fence? Or worse, to get loose and kill you and God knows who else before somebody put him down for good? You know how much he hated these things, can you honestly say he'd want to BE one?"

"Charlie wanted to live!" Sheila's voice trembled with tears. Carrie couldn't tell if they were tears of sorrow or pissoff, and she really didn't care which. She also didn't understand Joe's insistance upon getting Sheila's consent before putting a bullet in what was left of Charlie's brain. Not, she reflected, that Charlie had ever possessed much in the way of brains to begin with. If he had, he would have followed protocol and shot the goon on sight instead of dicking around playing some stupid macho game with it and getting himself bitten. He'd also have stayed with the group instead of sneaking away for some private shopping. He'd broken not one but two rules and as a consequence he was dead and she was stuck having this incredibly redundant discussion with this overblown twit.

Upon reflection, she thought that maybe Charlie had actually gained a few points on the old IQ scale by dying and forgetting to stay dead. Although if you followed that particular train of logic to its end you'd end up pitching Sheila into the run with Charlie, to see if a few bites could raise her IQ from its current level of moron up to something as exalted as village idiot.

At this point in time, though, Sheila was outside the dog run and planted firmly in the way of them doing what had to be done to keep their little community safe. Joe was the ranking officer at Ramon, and had opened the fort to all survivors. The only citizenship requirements were to stay alive long enough to get there, and abide by the rules that kept them all from becoming food for the undead masses waiting beyond the gates.

Carrie wondered with weary anger why, of all possible survivors, the duo of Sheila and Charlie had been among the lucky few to make it to Fort Ramon without becoming entrees. They wouldn't have managed it without help from Joe's soldiers, who had spotted the old Ford Charlie had been driving as it zig-zagged through Ramon park, pursued by several hundred ravenous zombies. Using rifles and flamethrowers, and at considerable personal risk, the troopers had held off the hoarde of walking dead long enough for them to get across the two mile stretch of park land and make it to the safety of the fort. She thought the numerous pets they'd saved were a much better return for the expended ammunition than Charlie and Sheila could ever be. At least the animals were grateful for the sanctuary, and they provided distraction and solace for the thirty seven children, mostly without parents, that the group had managed to rescue.

Charlie had been bitten during the last food run to the shopping center in Forest Hills and had concealed that little factoid from the rest of the group. Only Sheila had known, and in the brief period between Charlie succombing to his bite wound and reanimating with an improved IQ and an appetite for human flesh, Sheila had managed to drag his body outside and lock it in the dog run. Or maybe she'd dragged him out there while he was still alive. Carrie thought that scenario seemed more likely, given the brevity of the period between death and living death.

Joe was regarding Sheila with none of the anger or contempt that Carrie felt. All she could see in his face was sorrow and compassion. Not for the first time, she offered up a silent prayer to God thanking Him for making it Joe in charge of the fort when the world changed. If it had been one of the low forehead types, or Republican politicians, they'd have shut the gates tight against the civilian survivors and she and her son (and the five other kids Carrie had found hiding in Max's classroom when she had arrived at his school) would have been well and truly hosed.

Instead, Joe had opened the fort to all non-zombies, even those marginal cases like Sheila, Charlie, and the six survivors of the Bronx-based motorcycle gang who had arrived on their noisy choppers, stoned to the nines and roaring with laughter as they shot their way through to the fort. (Of course Joe had immediately relieved them of their weapons and drugs and locked them in the guardhouse until they were sober enough to understand and agree to abide by his rules. He'd also had the foresight to assign them all to different work details and shifts.)

Going even further, Joe had planned and led numerous rescue missions in the past months, slipping through the streets crowded with the ravenous undead, bringing any living thing, human or animal, back to the safety of the fort. He had once confided to Carrie that as a career military officer, he had been supported by taxpayer dollars all of his life. Therefore he saw it as his sacred duty to save as many taxpayer lives as he possibly could. Privately, Carrie thought it unlikely that Sheila, Charlie or the six bikers had ever paid taxes in their lives. Still, at least the bikers had proven to be hard workers and good fighters. Six out of eight wasn't bad.

Carrie herself had been a taxpayer before the change. Her contributions to the nations coffers had been financed by her job as an administrative assistant at Merril Lynch, which meant that she was used to following a CEO type around and seeing that his shoes were tied, his fly was zipped, and his directives were properly delegated.

Initially impressed with her rescue of the six children, Joe had learned to value her administrative and organizational abilities as well. She had quickly become his right hand man, helping him stay on top of the hundreds of day to day tasks involved in keeping the fort safe, acquiring supplies, and performing rescue missions. She also helped with his less pleasant duties, such as the task they were involved with this morning.

Joe was still speaking softly to Sheila, who had segued from angry yelling to strident wails while Carrie had been chasing her own thoughts. He had one arm around Sheila's shoulders and he offered her his handkerchief. Sheila was sobbing loudly, and she blew her nose with a great honking snort. Her white blonde hair, black at the roots, was still perfectly in place, hardened into a helmet atop her head with the application of a good half can of hairspray. Charlie had always pocketed several cans of hairspray for Sheila during their supply runs. In fact, the odds were good that on his last fatal mission Charlie had left the group for the express purpose of acquiring more of the stuff. Carrie guessed that in the near future Sheila was going to be exploring the scary world of laquer-free hairstyling. At this moment, Sheila's eye shadow and mascara were rather badly smeared, making her look like a cartoon version of a punk rock raccoon.

After several more minutes of ever-weakening protests Sheila finally stopped shaking her head in negation and managed to nod jerkily to Joe, although she still glared at Carrie. As if, Carrie thought, she had arranged for the goon to bite Charlie just to enjoy the sheer pleasure of this moment. Joe gently put an arm around Sheila's shaking shoulders and steered her toward the door that led to Ramon's main 'street'.

"Will you be ok handling this?" he asked Carrie over his shoulder. He shifted his eyes towards the back door and what waited in the yard. When she nodded he added, "I'm going to take Sheila over to where the people from that store we brought in last week are bunking and see if they can find an extra cot for her. I don't think she should have to stay here by herself after this." What he really meant, Carrie knew, was that this particular dwelling would hold up to six people comfortably and they needed the space.

Carrie waited until she heard the front door of the small house bang shut, then turned towards the back door and what waited for her out in the yard. She squared her small shoulders and stepped through the door, unslinging the shotgun from the strap that held it across her back. She preferred the accuracy and stopping power of the shotgun to either of the pistols she wore. Not to mention that they had a lot more shotgun shells stocked at Ramon than rounds for her smaller weapons.

As she stepped through the door, the thing that had been Charlie Vickers flung itself against its chain link prison with renewed vigor, bloody saliva drooling unnoticed from its lower lip. As it snarled at her it managed to spray the fence with what looked like partially masticated bits of its own tongue. One jaundiced eye was fixed on her, the other rolled wildly towards the roof of the dog run and the sky beyond.

Carrie allowed herself a moment of regret for Charlie. She had never liked him. Had, in fact, considered him a prime specimen of asshole, but he had been one of their small community and a living human being. Which had made him officially a member of an endangered species. Although Carrie didn't like Shiela either, Charlie had loved her and she had loved Charlie. The world had turned into a strange and hostile place almost overnight, and she guessed that things like love were in short supply. Love between people she didn't like was still love, after all, and she guessed that their diminished world was further diminished by its loss.

She shook her head, a quick gesture of negation. One day it might be her dead and disintegrating in a dog run, or Max, or any of the other five kids that bunked with them and that she'd come to regard as her own. As far as she knew, the whole planet was seething with hostile, ravenous corpses and sooner or later she'd screw up, or somebody else would screw up, and she'd get that bullet in the brain that meant game over, no replay.

The only real hope of winning was to stay alive until the new masters of the world had rotted beyond their ability to move and lay where they fell with their jaws snapping uselessly at the air. When that happened they'd be able to emerge from their fortress, killing the dead in relative safety. What would life be like, on a world literally covered with billions of decomposing human beings? She shook her head again. Concentrate on her children, and on the now, and face the future when it becomes the present. In the meantime, there was work to be done, wasn't there?

"Aw, shit," she mumbled, and to her surprise she felt tears on her face. She brought the shotgun up and settled the stock into the hollow of her shoulder. "Better karma next go-round, Charlie." She squinted through sudden tears as she trained the gun sight on the bridge of Charlie's nose, above the reeking mouth which was now attempting to bite through the chain link, bloody drool hanging in long runners from the battered chin.

She fired.

The Sort-of Suicide of a
Teenage Drama Queen

K. W. Koocher

There is no glamour to be found in death. That's the one truth that no teenager can manage to get through his or her thick skull to penetrate the adolescent brain beneath. Hell, you believed it yourself before you died, didn't you? Now, though, you know what dead people do. They decompose. The only thing in this world that they'll ever do again is stink.

Before you died, you used to think that there was something romantic and glorious about dying young. Your classmates stand in tight groups in the funeral parlor, casting spurious sideways glances towards your coffin, all of them red-eyed and snuffling. Everybody talks about you in hushed whispers, recalling every time they saw you; what they said, what you said. You're suddenly more popular than the quarterback. They dedicate the yearbook 'in memory of' you. Wowsa, recognition at last!

For a day or two. Within a week, you're in the ground and they've replaced you as editor of the school paper, a new kid is sitting at your desk in computer club, and the quarterback has stopped telling stories about how you helped him in math. Instead, he has returned to his hobby of banging that bitch Heather McDarmid in the back seat of the car Daddy gave her for Christmas.

Within a year, only the newspaper and computer geeks can recall what you looked like. Within five years, everybody has left any memory of you behind in the hallowed halls of high school and they've moved on. Most went to college, but some started families. Good old Heather is already making a fortune at some bullshit job in Daddy's company. The quarterback is now a used car salesman with the start of male pattern baldness and two kids cementing him forever to that shrew he knocked up after Heather dumped him.

You're frozen in time. You died in high school and the world didn't end. Even your mother stopped getting all misty-eyed at the sound of your name. That picture of you that she keeps on the piano actually has dust on it.

You've become a statistic, another teenage suicide linked to Goth-ism, the occult and heavy metal music. This connection was made because you owned three black t-shirts, one CD of The Greatest Metal Bands of All Time, and a star-shaped dark purple candle. You were still shy, even though your braces had come off a year ago and your skin had cleared up. Combined with the evidence of your meager possessions, shy equated to withdrawn, a lingering reluctance to smile became evidence of sullenness. Of course you committed suicide. You had been showing all of the warning signs, hadn't you?

In the weeks following your burial there was a lot of ranting about metal music and teenage suicide. Nobody mentioned the living death that is the natural state of kids like you. Every school has a few, those outcast children who scuttle through the halls with their heads tucked between their shoulders, the great hoards of the never-there. Teachers know that they can call upon you in class if they're stuck for a student who has actually read the assignment, but none of them ever really speak to you. Not their job.

All of this you watch from the shadows as you linger after your sudden and painful separation from your physical self. You could go any time, but you stubbornly cling to these streets, your house, this town. The sight of your broken, frail body as the policemen pull you from the river moves you to tears that you can't shed. Above you, a white light constantly beckons, around you the world still spins. You, though, you're dead and buried and the son-of-a-bitch that killed you is still walking around and his life is going on just like everybody else's. Well, everybody else's but yours. You're decomposing.

You follow him, shouting in your unheard voice to your mother, to your teachers, even to the quarterback. Nobody hears you, nobody alive anyway. Your fellow dead hear you, they just don't care. Even the two other girls you watch the son-of-a-bitch kill, while your fists pass harmlessly through his body and your unheard screams fill the night, don't care. They just throw their arms wide and are taken, smiling, into that compellingly beautiful white light.

Why do you stay in this hellish state of Limbo? Is this state of non-being easier for you than for the others because you were hardly there even when you were alive? Five years of effort and you have yet to make anybody even feel a chill when you hover in the same space they occupy, but still you stubbornly cling to this world trying to somehow stop the son-of-a-bitch.

The light calls, beckoning you. It hints at acceptance, recognition, even love. You were never actually loved, you think. You weren't real enough to love. You were real for three days, and you spent those days lying in state as classmates trooped by to peer curiously at your dead face and your older relatives whispered to each other that the undertaker had made you look "very good" and "lifelike". You make a note to self: Next life request a closed casket topped by a photograph, because this just blows.

You see a stranger in the coffin, somebody who looks so unlike you that you check the name posted at the door of the viewing room that your light blue casket occupies. Of course it's blue, you hated blue. To you, the girl in the coffin looks ready for her big screen debut, not for the box to be closed and dirt to be shoveled down into the hole in which she will get on with the business of decomposing. Skin color obscured by pancake makeup, cheeks rouged, lips ruby red, they even make your eyelashes thicker somehow. All of the bruised and broken places are skillfully covered over and concealed, and is that actually cotton balls packing your cheeks? "Eeeewwww, Gross!" would have been the comment of the alive version of you. You know this because it is the comment of the dead version of you.

"If only, if only..." The litany chases itself around your non-corporeal brain for days at a time. "If only I hadn't liked the view of downtown from that damned bridge so much. If only I could make myself seen, heard, felt by SOMEBODY, we could nail the son-of-a-bitch and I could go and maybe, just maybe, finally be happy. If only I'd had one friend who knew me well enough to know the last God damned thing I'd ever do in this world would be to fling myself off a bridge."

But that's the trouble, isn't it? Everybody thinks that the last God damned thing you ever did in this world was to fling yourself off a bridge. It's painful to realize that they believe you were enough of an idiot to pull a drama queen stunt like that. Even more insulting, that you'd pull a drama queen stunt like that and not leave a long tearful note, full of adolescent angst and a pathetic attempt at bravery, parceling your meager possessions out to the few kids who would actually speak to you.

Jesus, Mary and Joseph, Heather actually weeps at your funeral! Popular, beautiful Heather, the richest girl in town, whose interactions with you in the seven years you attended the same school consisted almost entirely of breaking into giggles with her girlfriends when you walked past the cafeteria table where she always held court.

Certainly, you think, if there were any justice she'd have been knocked ass over teakettle by the son-of-a-bitch and then picked up and thrown bodily from the bridge instead of you. Never mind that it's evil to think such thoughts. You're already dead and stuck in this hellish limbo so what does it matter what you think? Unlike you, Heather deserved it. She of the cutting quip who sheds crocodile tears at your funeral and never noticed you were alive, unless she needed a target for one of her jibes.

Ironic, then, that the day you finally stop the son-of-a-bitch, the life you save is Heather's. Maybe it isn't irony at all, maybe it is because you acted to save the one you hated instead of stepping aside and watching her die. You don't really know.

What you do know is that you happen to be haunting Heather on that particular evening, hovering not five feet away as she is standing on the same bridge in the same spot you stopped at to gaze at the city skyline, and she is crying. You wonder what Heather could possibly have to cry about. You think that this is classic Heather, posed dramatically on the bridge to shed her sorrowful tears against the breathtaking nighttime backdrop of the glowing city.

So perfect is the picture she makes that when you

first hear the footsteps you're sure that they're made by the feet of a handsome prince, who will undoubtedly sweep Heather into his arms to commence the next fairy-tale chapter in the fairy-tale saga that is the Life of Heather.

This image is so disgusting that you turn away, deciding to haunt rats in the city dump or cockroaches in a trash bin or anything that will be less nauseating than seeing Heather swept into the arms of her next Prince Charming.

Then memory and understanding penetrate the cloud of irritation in your incorporeal brain and you recognize that sound of gravel underfoot. You know it because it is branded into your memory as the last sound the alive version of you ever heard and as you whirl back towards Heather your only thought is, "Oh no you don't!"

Somehow your fingers close on Heather's sleeve and you yank her to one side just before the son-of-a-bitch hits her. His momentum carries him past Heather and because he plans to hit her with every pound of his not inconsiderable weight he sails right over the railing. Down he soars, like a certain teenage girl did five years ago, screaming the whole way, hitting the water with a loud splat-splash. Isn't it wonderful?

Or is the wonderful part standing on the bank of the river watching as his ghost - or spirit or whatever you are in that time between death and moving on - wades out of that filthy river, looking so befuddled and terrified?

Or is the wonderful part when the light surrounds him? Not a white light like you see above you but an oozing black un-light that seeps into his nose and ears and mouth as he screams and screams and slowly fades away, becoming one with that hideously wrong light and shrieking through every long second of the process.

Or is the wonderful part going back to your mother's house and gazing at her sleeping form one last time, silently forgiving her for not loving you enough or not believing in you or letting your picture get dusty as she picked up the reins of life without you? You go up to the attic and rummage until you find Teddy, who slept with you every night of your life, even on the day camp overnights and your trip to Disney World. You're grateful for your mother's obliviousness for once - if she had actually noticed how you felt about Teddy he'd probably have been rotting in your coffin, your dead arms clasped about him and firmly held together with wire or duct tape or something.

With no difficulty, you scoop Teddy into your arms, holding his threadbare body tightly against you and saying to the white light, "Ok, I'm ready now."

The white light brightens to fill the room, and suddenly it is filling you. It doesn't bring cold agony, like the black light brought the son-of-a-bitch. You throw your head back, the better to inhale it, and Oh God it is so warm and you're safe, and for the first time you understand love because you've become love.

The white light fills you, then it takes you. Isn't it wonderful?

The Strange Nuclear Prophecy of Kittens

K. W. Koocher

The kitten finally died at 3:00 am, and Terry wept as she wrapped the small body in plastic and consigned it to the freezer in the basement. She had known that it would more than likely die, but she had nonetheless labored to keep the poor pathetic thing alive.

She had found it in the morning. She had awakened not long after Jack had left for his ten hours at the plant. Her first stop of the day had of course been a pit stop, then she had meandered down the driveway to the mailbox to pick up the morning paper. On her way back to the house she had seen Clara the cat stalking across the lawn, tail twitching in anticipation as she headed for the bowl that Terry kept for her on the front porch. Clara had looked decidedly thinner than usual, and Terry realized that she must have finally delivered her kittens.

Arriving at the house, Terry had found the trap in the far corner of the porch, right where she had carefully set it the night before. It sat tilted onto one side, sprung and of course completely innocent of occupation, the dish of food with which she had baited it upside-down and empty. Clara had appeared on their porch three weeks ago, looking very bedraggled and more than slightly pregnant. Jack, always soft hearted, had run to town for a bag of cat food, and Clara had been hanging around ever since. Terry had rented the trap from Valley Humane two days before, hoping to catch Clara before she delivered. Terry hated the thought of the kittens growing up to be strays, and both she and Jack had taken a liking to Clara. They'd been talking about getting a cat when Clara had appeared. Almost, Terry thought, like a little gift from God.

In disgust, she retrieved the empty food bowl from the trap. She stared balefully at the trap for a long moment, then turned it on end and leaned it against the porch railing with a muttered, "Foolproof my foot!" She fished a small bag of cat food from the bin on the porch and re-filled the bowl. She set the bowl down, casting the foolproof but not Claraproof trap a final resigned glance.

"Can't catch you now, Sweetie," she said to Clara, who sat waiting a safe distance away, her beautiful green eyes following Terry's every move. "Don't want your babies to starve without you."

Terry replaced the bag of food in the bin and closed it firmly. As she walked back to the front door, Clara rushed to the bowl, settling down to eat her breakfast. Terry saluted the cat, then opened the door. The kittens must be in the tool shed. She'd look for them later, she decided, and leave a box and some old towels for Clara to bed down with them in. As Terry was about to cross the threshold, a slight movement at the other corner of the large, old-fashioned porch attracted her attention.

Terry let the door close and crossed to the corner opposite the happily munching Clara, awkwardly bending over for a closer look. Face down on the bare floor boards, a tiny white shape struggled feebly. With a start, Terry realized that the minuscule creature was a newborn kitten.

For a moment she was nonplused. She thought she remembered being told that you shouldn't touch a baby animal, that if you do its mother will reject it and it will die. Looking around, she saw no other kittens. From the size Clara had been this morning, there was no way in the world that this tiny thing had been her only offspring. Furthermore there was no blood or any kind of bedding where this kitten was lying, and it was way too young and weak to have crawled up on the porch by itself. Clara must have put it here and kept the others wherever her nest was. For some reason Clara had rejected this one kitten.

Awkwardly, Terry stretched down and picked the tiny thing up. Turning it over in her hand, her first look at the kitten's face caused her to gasp in shock and revulsion. The kitten was horribly deformed.

Where Clara had two very normal emerald eyes, one on either side of her rather pert black nose, her kitten had only one single huge black eye, located in the center of its face. As far as Terry could see, the kitten had no nose or nostrils, only a smooth bump below its single staring eye. It seemed to be breathing with some effort, mouth open, tiny chest rising and falling.

Slowly Terry raised her horrified gaze from the small thing in her hand, her eyes drawn almost involuntarily to the three cooling towers, slightly hazy and shimmering in the late morning sunshine. The Springfield Valley Power Company's main plant was less than five miles from her house, dominating the skyline above the valley where the small town of Springfield lay spread out at the feet of the immense towers. Almost like a sacrifice, she thought, not for the first time.

Visibly and invisibly, the nuclear plant defined the valley. Everybody in town worked there, or had a family member who worked there. Springfield Power had repeatedly assured the townspeople that the plant was safe, in meetings held when the plant was first proposed and in its ubiquitous newsletters since the plant had come on-line two years ago. Roy Brannigan, Springfield Valley mayor and the richest man in town, waxed eloquent on the subject of plant safeguards whenever questioned by any of his constituents. And now here was this kitten, born almost in the shadow cast by the tall towers. Great.

Terry took the kitten inside and made a bed for it in an old cardboard carton, wrapping a heating pad in a towel to place in the box and laying the kitten gently upon the towel. She found the can of kitten milk substitute and the bottle that Jack had bought with his usual "I'm covering all possibilities" attitude after they had realized Clara was going to have kittens. After the kitten showed no ability to suckle from the bottle, she began feeding it with an eye dropper, just a small amount every hour. The instructions on the milk substitute stated rather emphatically that overfeeding a kitten was something to be avoided.

Despite her best efforts, the kitten grew steadily weaker throughout the afternoon and evening. Jack called at six to tell her that he was stuck doing a double, covering for a co-worker who had called in sick at the Plant. After less than a minute of conversation - with his usual uncanny perception - he said that he thought she sounded a little upset and asked if he should he come home early anyway. Terry told him not to worry, everything was fine. She was upset because Clara had delivered her kittens in the woodshed, that was all. Stay at work, we can sure use the extra ten hours of double time. Jack had laughed and agreed, and hung up after extracting a promise to call him if she needed to.

Terry went to bed at 10:00 pm, setting her alarm for 11:00, then for 12:00, then for 1:00. When she woke at 3:00 and checked the kitten, the little creature was cold and stiff. That was when she began to cry. After carefully wrapping the tiny body and consigning it to the freezer, she went out onto the porch. In the cold darkness she sat on the big swing, huddled in a blanket and gazing through her tears at the lights of the plant so close to her home.

She sat there for a long time, her mood a strange mixture of panic and resignation. She sat and she rocked, the tears still coming, thinking of pretty Clara and the little kitten with the single monstrous staring eye. As she rocked, she gazed at the plant, her hands absently stroking her own gravid belly.

The Positive Power of Preyer

K. W. Koocher

People ask me sometimes - and it's always people who think they're Christians but aren't really Right with the Lord or they'd already know - they ask me why me and Sylvie have so many children. As if any real Christian would have to ask such a darned stupid thing.

Sylvie and me, we have fifteen kids because we love each other, and because God has blessed us and showered His blessings on our love. That's the plain and simple truth of the matter. Anything else is just lies, the work of Satan himself trying to worm his way into our lives like the Serpent did in the Garden of Eden.

Sylvie is my wife, we met back in 1992 when I did a revival show in Pottboro, Arizona, a little town just on the edge of the Kohatchee Indian Reservation. I was 35 then, and newly Baptized in the Lord, but filled with the Holy Spirit of our Lord and Savior Christ Jesus Almighty. I lived and traveled in a smallish Airstream camper that I had filled with Biblical Tracts proclaiming the Word of the One True God and His Only Son Jesus Christ. I would set up a tent to preach in and use a tape recording for my organ music. It was nothin' fancy, like those sinnin' TV preachers gots, but the Lord God would speak through me as His Voice and His Instrument and the people would listen and hear His Word.

Sylvie came to the revival show alone, oh her people was fearful sinners. But the Holy Spirit was working in her, and she'd snuck out to hear the Word, Praise God. After the service was over, she knocked on the door of my traveling home. She was fifteen years old then, and untouched. I knew before I threw open the door that the Lord God Almighty had sent to me the Wife that I had prayed to him for.

We said our vows before God that night, our hands resting on the Real Leather Bound Bible with Gilt Pages and the Words of our Lord in Red that I did my preaching out of. When we paid our call on her people in the morning, our first seed was already planted and growing in her belly. That was as it is supposed to be. The Wife is a Vessel for the Holy Seed of her Husband, and from his loins is produced the fruits of our Lord's love.

Sylvie's mamma and her daddy was fearful sinners, like I said, not Right in the eyes of the Lord God Almighty. They gnashed their teeth and spoke with the Tongues of Serpents the morning after our Holy Joining, but let not the Children of God be undone by the voices of demons. In the end they, too, were purified in the eyes of the Lord.

After we had laid them to rest, we took from them only what we needed. Sylvie was the eldest child and the inheritor of all of their worldly goods. We did not need their home, as we planned to live in mine, which was proper. The Wife shall leave the home of her Father and care for the home of her Husband. Sylvie and me was charged with the Most Holy Mission, to continue to preach the Word of the Lord God.

As Sylvie's husband I was charged with the guardianship of all that was hers, it is not the place of a woman to own properties or have dealings with any man besides the husband she cleaves herself to. Sylvie is a good Christian woman, and confines herself to those matters that are a woman's province, leaving to me the business of a man.

I chose to bequeath her parents' home to her infant

brother. We left the babe sleeping in his crib while we read the Scriptures over the fresh graves in the woods behind the house. Then Sylvie left her father's house forever, to join with her husband as we drove away to begin our new lives of spreading the Word of God together.

Our first son we named Caleb, a goodly and God-fearing sort of name. Our second boy we called Seth. Then we had a girl, Elizabeth. Our fourth child was also a girl, and we named her Ruth.

After Elizabeth was born, we realized that we were outgrowing our home. Me and Sylvie prayed mightily upon this matter, and the Lord did provide. In a deserted winter campground in Wyoming we happened upon two men, committing the Sin of Sodomy. When they would not repent of their wickedness, the Lord God charged us to scourge them of their wrongnesses. After we had done so, and given them Christian Burial - for, at the last, they had Repented, as all Sodomites shall do when confronted with the wrath of the Lord God Almighty - we found among their possessions a key, which led us to their lodgings at a small inn in town.

We Purified and Cleansed their room with Scripture and blessed Holy Water, since it had been the scene of sin. Among the gifts there that the Lord did bestow upon us was another key, this one to the Motor Home that we conduct our ministry from unto this day. The rest of the Sinners' belongings we gave unto the charity box in town, for so the Lord God tells us, that we shall not suffer a surfeit of worldly goods, but that instead all the Kingdom of God shall be given to he who gives away all that he has.

And so we travel this beautiful Country of God

unto this day. I choose our path as God sets my course along the highways in the beautiful Home that He has provided for us. Our ten sons travel with me, that I may teach them in the ways of the Lord God, Father to Son, as is proper and written in the scriptures.

Sylvie follows behind us in our first home, which we kept, for it is written that waste is a Sin in the Eyes of God. Our five daughters travel with their Mother, and she instructs them in the proper place and role of a Daughter of the Kingdom. Sylvie is again great with child, soon her time will grow nigh and our love will again be blessed.

Last summer Caleb, who is 15, took to him a Wife. Her family had named her Brittany, which was a Sinful name, but she has been Christened Mary in the eyes of the Lord. She had been Cast Out by her parents, and Caleb met her when she embraced the Lord God at a Revival meeting we held outside of Los Angeles. The path our Lord God has set our feet upon leads us slowly South and East. When we reach the home of Mary's family we will call upon them, to assure them that their Daughter is well and properly Wed and Right with the Lord God our Father. We will give them a chance to Repent of their evil, and Scourge the Taint of Satan from them.

Throughout our Ministry, the Lord has been present in our lives and our family has prospered in Love and Faith. Whenever we have hungered, He has fed us. Whenever we were naked, He has clothed us. Whenever we thirsted, He gave us to drink. Whatever our needs, the Lord has always provided in abundance. There is no shortage of Sinners, and the Souls we have Saved are Legion.

I see the cities and this modern world of technology and wonders. I think that they are joyless places, the lives within them empty and suffering. At the tent Services, as I gaze from the pulpit at my own family, bound together by Trust and Sacrifice and our Mission from the Lord Jesus himself, I cannot help but pity those we pass by.

I sometimes wish that I could show them, Share with them, the plain secret to the happiness and deep love that Sylvie and I live every day with our children. It's very simple, really. The family that Preys Together, Stays Together.

Down to One

K. W. Koocher

The sounds of Jacob's labored breathing had finally ceased. Consciousness had fled nearly ten minutes ago. Now life had fled as well. He had been pale and sick within minutes of being bitten. Five hours later, he had slipped into his final coma.

Candy pulled her gun from her belt. She had dragged Jacob up 65 flights of stairs to this posh office - complete with lovely outside terrace - that had once hosted some long-dead executroid. Jacob had wanted to feel the sun warming his body before he died.

She racked a round into the chamber as Jacob lunged to his feet. His intelligent blue eyes were now cloudy and puke colored and empty. He snarled, and her bullet caught him squarely on the bridge of his nose, vaporizing the top of his head. His body flew backwards and flipped over the railing, cart wheeling through the air. She was up too high to hear his final impact on the street below. She kissed her wedding band as her tears streaked her cheeks in the late afternoon sunshine.

Christmas Dinner With Liz and Jim

K. W. Koocher

Liz turned off the burner, and carefully poured the soup into the 'for special' soup bowls. She laid a circle of cheese over each bowl, then slid the bowls into the microwave and thumbed the "Minute Plus" button. She turned to grab a tray as the querulous voice spoke yet again from the dining room.

"Is that soup almost ready?" Jim asked, for what seemed like the twentieth time. "I'm starving."

"Yep, coming right in," Liz replied, as the microwave beeped. She scooped the bowls onto the tray, the cheese beautifully melted over the top of each serving of onion soup, just like in a fancy restaurant.

Liz carried the tray carefully from the kitchen into the dining room, where Jim sat at the head of the festively decorated Christmas Dinner table. There was a huge turkey, beautifully done to a perfect golden brown. Next to the turkey was a big bowl of stuffing, made with apple bits and raisins the way Jim liked it. There was a dish of cranberries, a bowl of gravy and a loaf of brown bread next to a plate of real butter. There was a bowl of candied yams made with brown sugar, mashed potatoes and green beans.

Liz paused in the doorway, looking at the table laden with the feast she had spent all day cooking. She had worked until two the night before, getting home just before three. Jim hadn't been home yet, in fact he hadn't come home for the past six nights. Liz had fallen gratefully into bed, only to be awakened by Jim's arrival at a quarter to five, dead drunk and demanding a "real man's breakfast".

Liz had gotten up and started throwing together

some pancakes. "No," Jim had whined. "I want a real breakfast. Pancakes and bacon and eggs and potatoes and coffee and orange juice."

Liz had recognized the danger signals, and silently complied. Five in the morning, after working a double shift at the diner until two, and here she was cooking enough breakfast for an army of lumberjacks. Better to be tired than black and blue, though. So she had cooked. Jim had staggered away from the table after downing all of the food, falling into sodden sleep in a diagonal sprawl across the bed. Liz had washed and dried the dishes, put them away, then gone to finish her interrupted sleep on the couch, the alarm set for eight so she could get up in plenty of time to prepare their Christmas feast.

That had been her Christmas Eve, and now it was Christmas Day. Jim had demanded a big traditional Christmas Dinner, telling her to cook enough for his sister and brother-in-law, their three kids, his mother, his father - plus the father's girlfriend - his brother and his brother's latest girlfriend. She wasn't to invite her family, not that she would have anyway. Whenever she thought of her parents seeing the way she was living, she was deeply ashamed.

None of his family had shown up, of course. She had known before starting to cook that none of them were coming. His sister kept her kids as far from their Uncle Jim as she possibly could, there was no way she would have come to their place for dinner, especially a memorable event like Christmas Dinner. Jim's father was probably dead drunk and fighting with his equally drunk girlfriend. Jim's mother was probably dead drunk and crying in her beer about the father having a girlfriend.

Jim's brother was doubtless putting it to his latest skank in some roach motel, and the odds were they were dead drunk as well.

I hate him, she suddenly realized, looking at Jim. Clearly seeing, perhaps for the first time, the broken veins and puffy skin that marred his once-handsome face. His mouth, which she had once seen as "drop-dead gorgeous" was turned down at the corners in its usual petulant pout. His once beautiful blue eyes now looked small and piggish, glazed with the remnants of a six-day drunk, bloodshot and dangerous as they shifted about, ready to recognize some excuse, however piss-poor, to go off on her so he could break dance on her face with his fists, then get drunk again because "that bitch is driving me to it".

"Hurry up with that soup, Woman," he demanded, trying to sound jocular and only succeeding in sounding peevish. "Your man is hungry!"

Oh fuck you, Liz thought, as she hurried forward to set his soup down in front of him. *Fuck you, choke on it and I hope you die.*

He smiled at her as he caught sight of the soup, French Onion au Gratin, prepared just as he liked it in the fancy bowls he had stolen from work the last time he had a job. Later, Liz decided that it was the smile that had done it. Just one straw too many for old camel Liz, that smile.

"Here's your fucking soup, you COCKSUCKER!" she shrieked, and swept her hands forward, hurling both bowls of hot soup into his face. "Here's your fucking soup and I hope you fucking CHOKE on it!"

Jim roared in pain and rage as both bowls of soup

bounced into his lap. He leapt to his feet, his chair clattering to the floor behind him.

"You fucking BITCH!" he yelled. "Have you lost your mind?"

Liz dropped the tray and snatched the coffee pot from the table. Jim always insisted that a pot of coffee be on the table at every meal. Liz hated coffee.

"You forgot your fucking coffee!" she shrieked, and let him have the pot squarely on the bridge of his nose. He was immediately soaked with blood as his nose collapsed, the bone and cartilage - still fragile from being rebuilt after his last bar fight - disintegrating under the metal rim of the pot. Hot coffee sprayed into his face, burning its way quickly down his body.

Liz spun, still holding the pot, and followed her initial blow with a harder one to the side of his head. With a look of stupid surprise he stumbled backwards, and she swung again, this time shattering the metal pot on the top of his head. He sat down with a grunt, missing his chair and falling to the floor.

"Oh you bitch," he growled thickly. "You fucking bitch."

"Here's your fucking turkey!" Liz screamed. She plucked the bird from the table, holding it up over her head by both legs. "Merry Christmas, you fucking prick!"

She swung the turkey downward with all of her might. There was a thick squishing sound as bird met skull. Skull won the initial round, but, Liz realized, bird won the battle. She stepped back, staring in dumb amazement. Jim's head was gone, having been swallowed by the enormous bird. The turkey rested on Jim's

100

shoulders, his head and neck buried inside the former Christmas dinner. The wings flopped on Jim's shoulders, the legs waved from where the top of Jim's head bulged inside the bird.

Jim went purely crazy. That was the only way Liz could describe it. He flailed uselessly at the turkey for a moment, then lurched to his feet. He staggered two steps, running into the table and nearly knocking it over. Turning, he ran in the opposite direction, bouncing off of the wall, then turning again and caroming off of the other wall.

Finally, he found the door, racing out into the hall as Liz stared after him, her anger and terror giving way to helpless spasms of almost hysterical laughter. There were several more thumps from the hallway, then a series of loud bangs.

"Guess he found the steps," she said in a shaky voice she hardly recognized as her own. She walked into the living room and picked up the telephone, punching in 911 with trembling fingers.

"I'm going to need an ambulance," she managed to gasp to the operator. She was still giggling helplessly. "My boyfriend appears to have had a wee bit too much Christmas turkey."

Anthony Marchionda, Jr.

Anthony Marchionda, Jr. was born and raised in Youngstown, Ohio. After graduating Cum Laude from Youngstown State University, he moved to Chicago. Over the next 13 years he pursued an acting career. Anthony moved to New York in the early 1990's and appeared in an Off Broadway play. He later moved back to Youngstown, Ohio.

Anthony has written three full-length screenplays and one short, as well as a book of short stories titled "Writers Cramp and Other Short Stories."

Writer's Cramp*

Anthony Marchionda, Jr.

* "Writer's Cramp" received Honorable Mention in the Best of Ohio Writer 2005 Contest.

" 'As Detective Matt Maloy placed the handcuffs on Lady Winterly's dainty wrists, he looked into her emerald green eyes and said, …' "

" '…He looked into her emerald green eyes and said, …' "

"He looked and he said, …"

"I haven't a friggin' clue as to what this jerk said," Paul shouted, as he yanked the paper out of the typewriter, crumpled it up and threw it in the wastebasket. "I hate it. One more line, just one more and I'm through with this damn story."

"I hate this story," Paul said, popping a cigarette between his lips. "I should have never started this damn thing."

Paul walked over to the stove and used the gas burner to light his cigarette.

"Okay, just stay calm. You can do this," he said, pacing across the floor of his cramped studio apartment.

"Shit," he said, looking at the wall clock in the kitchen. "Twenty minutes until the FedEx guy gets here to pick up the manuscript."

"Damn, it. Damn, it. Damn, it. What does he say? What does this moron say to her?"

Paul walked over to the kitchen counter and tore open a bag of Oreo cookies. He grabbed a handful of Oreos and continued pacing the floor. "What does he like about her? Okay, that's a start. What does he like about her that he might comment on." Paul ate several Oreos as the ideas bounced around inside his head.

"Matt Maloy looked into her emerald green eyes and

said, ...nice shoes!"

Paul slumped into the threadbare recliner chair, his head buried in his hands. "Oh God, this is terrible. My brain is frozen and I can't find the words. I should have become a dentist like my cousin Ernie."

Paul rocked back and forth. "Coffee, I need more coffee. That'll do it."

Paul pulled himself out of the recliner. He grabbed the coffee cup from his desk and walked back into the kitchen. He threw some instant coffee into his cup, added tap water and shoved the cup in the microwave. As he waited for the coffee to heat up, he paced over to the dartboard hanging on his closet door. He grabbed a dart and whipped it across the room. The dart impaled a picture of Paul's publisher, Sol Lipschitz, right between the eyes, and shattered the glass frame.

"You," Paul yelled, charging towards the picture. "It's all your fault, you rat bastard. You and your deadlines. How can you put a deadline on creativity? Did Michelangelo have a deadline? Did Van Gogh have a deadline?"

"One day," Paul said, wagging his finger at Sol's picture. "Mark my words. One of these days, the worm will turn and you will get yours."

The microwave dinged.

"Coffee, I need coffee."

Paul raced over to the microwave. He gently took out the coffee cup and blew a cooling breath over the healing elixir. He gingerly sipped from the cup, then leaned up against the kitchen counter. "Oh, that's good," he said. He lazily took a deep drag from his cigarette and slowly exhaled. "That's even better," he said.

Paul stared at the typewriter across the room. He put the cigarette in the corner of his mouth and resolutely walked towards the typewriter. He gently placed the coffee cup on top of the dozens of coffee rings that patterned his desk. He reached over to the stack of clean, white, 22-pound typing paper and lovingly took a sheet. With exacting precision, he placed the paper in the typewriter roller. He took one last drag on his cigarette then crushed it in the overly full ashtray.

Paul leaned in towards the typewriter and began typing.

" 'As Detective Matt Maloy placed the handcuffs on Lady Winterly's dainty wrists, he looked into her emerald green eyes and said, 'Love is a funny thing. It can happen when you least expect it, and with the person you hadn't even considered. I know it'll be tough on you, sugar. It'll be tough on me too. But, when you get out of prison, I'll be at the gate waitin' for you. No matter how long you're in for, I'll wait for you, baby.'

As the policeman put Lady Winterly into the patrol car, Matt flipped up the collar of his trench coat and walked down the street into the night.' "

"The end," Paul shouted, taking the final page out of the typewriter and putting it with the rest of the manuscript.

Paul grabbed a large yellow post-it notepad and a felt tipped pen. He began to write.

" 'Dear Sol,

Enclosed, you will find my latest manuscript titled, 'Lies Never Die.'

Thank you for all your support and encouragement.

Best regards,

Paul

P.S. Please send me a new picture of you. It seems that there has been another accident.' "

At that moment, the doorbell rang. "FedEx, right on time," Paul said, putting his manuscript inside the overnight delivery envelope.

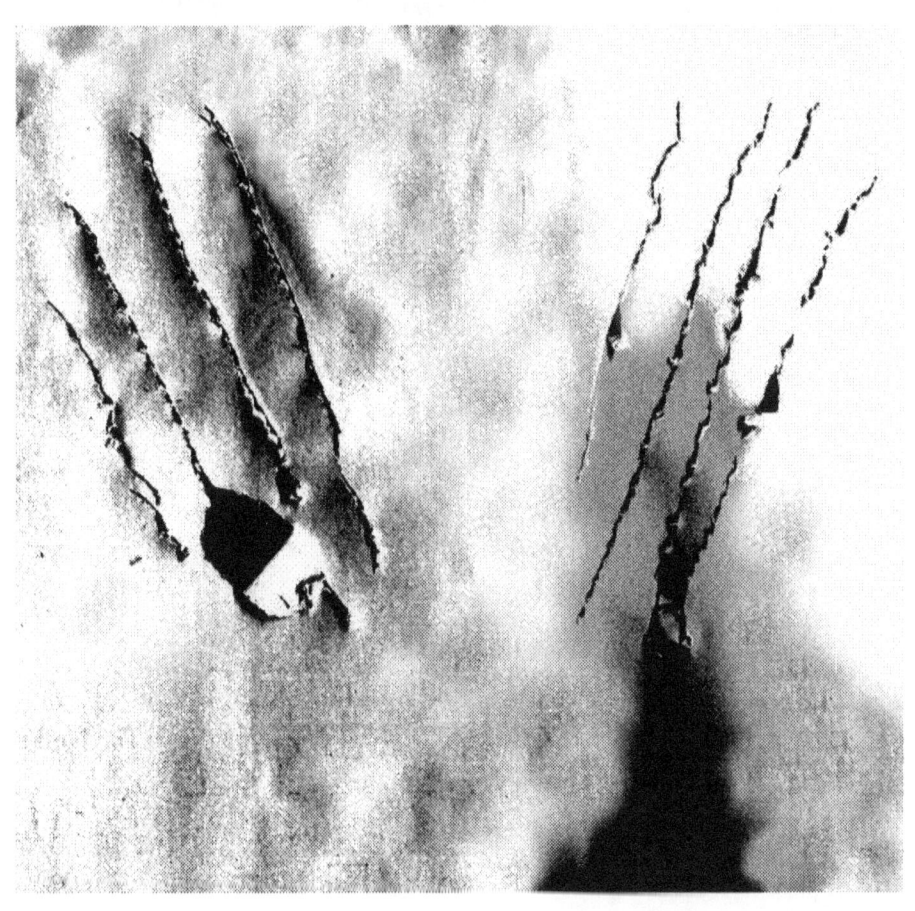

Animal Behavior

Anthony Marchionda, Jr.

"So, you're new here, huh?" Cat asked, as he circled around Dog

"Yes, Dog just get here," Dog said.

"So, how do you like it so far?" Cat asked.

"People, they nice to, Dog. They feed, Dog. They give Dog nice warm blanket to sleep on."

"Sure, they're nice to you *now*, but wait a few more days. I've been here a long time. I've seen things. Things they did to other canines that lived here."

"What…what they do?" Dog asked.

"I don't know, maybe I shouldn't tell you."

"Tell me, tell me. Dog want to know."

"Maybe it won't happen to you. Maybe it was just the last two mongrels that were here."

"No, please, you tell, Dog."

"Well…all right. Here's how it goes. The Man and Woman take you from this house while the Boy and Girl are in school. They drop you off at the Veterinarian, where you stay overnight."

"Yes, yes, I stay overnight. Then what?"

"Then the next day the Woman picks you up from the Veterinarian, carries you into the house in a brand new soft, furry dog bed, and places you down next to the warm, cozy fireplace."

"That sound nice. Dog like that."

"Oh sure, it's nice and cozy for *you*, but your balls are still at the Vet's office, in a jar, on a shelf somewhere."

With that revelation, Dog's eyes widened. He

backed up into a corner and crouched down on all fours.

"No, no, this not be true. People, *nice* people. People take Dog from street. Give Dog home."

"Well, believe whatever you want to believe, pal. All I can tell you is what I've seen happen around here. I'm just glad I'm a cat and not a dog," Cat said, licking his fur. "I wouldn't want to be in your shoes, er- I mean, paws."

"What is Dog to do? What is Dog to do?" Dog repeated, as he raced around the house from door to door, trying to get out. As Dog scratched at the kitchen door, Cat sauntered over to him.

"Cool your jets, Fido. All the doors are locked. They lock them every night before they go to bed. There's no way out."

"Please, help me. Please hide me. You cat, you smart. You think of something."

"No, wouldn't work, you're too big to hide. Sorry, you're on your own."

"No, please. Dog beg you. Dog do whatever Cat say. Help Dog, please."

"Well, there's only one way out of this, as far as I can see."

"Yes, talk more. Cat, talk more."

"Well, if you really want to make sure that you don't get sent to the Veterinarian…"

"Yes-yes?" Dog asked.

"You're going to have to kill them."

"Kill them?" Dog paused.

"Yes, in their sleep, tonight," Cat stated.

114

"You want Dog to kill Man and Woman?"

"Oh, not just the Man and the Woman, but the Boy and the Girl as well. You must understand that they are people. And people send their dogs to the Veterinarian. It is in their nature. You must get rid of *all* of them, or you will be sent to the Veterinarian."

"But, how? Dog not have weapon."

"Sure you do. A big brute like you, you've got the greatest weapon that nature ever created. Your big canine fangs," Cat exclaimed.

"My fangs?"

"Yes, your fangs."

"But how?" Dog asked.

"Oh, for the love of… I know you're a dog, but do I have to explain everything to you?"

Dog just stood there with a blank look on his face.

Cat took a deep breath and slowly let it out.

"Okay, here is what you do," Cat began. "You quietly climb up the stairs to the second floor. You go into the master bedroom. You then pounce on the Man, and with one quick bite to the Man's neck, you sever his jugular. You then do the same thing to the Woman. You quickly run to the Boy's room and do the same thing to him. Finally, you race to the Girl's room, before she can wake up, and do away with her the same way."

"I don't know," Dog wondered. "You sure this only way?"

"Hey, look. Do whatever you want to do. They're your nuts, not mine."

Dog closed his eyes and thought for a moment.

"Dog, do it."

"Good for you, Dog," Cat said, as he ambled over to the refrigerator. Mark my words, when you're through, your troubles will be over."

Dog lowered his head and quietly made his way up the stairs to the second floor. As growls and screams pierced the air, Cat wedged his fat, furry rump against the refrigerator door and popped it open. Cat perused the contents of the refrigerator as if it were a smorgasbord.

"Hmm, lets see what's in *this* bowl," Cat said, as he knocked a big plastic bowl from one of the refrigerator shelves. "Tuna salad, my favorite," Cat exclaimed, as the contents of the bowl splattered onto the kitchen floor.

"Those silly people. To think that they actually had the nerve to bring another pet into *my* home," Cat thought to himself, as he licked the tuna salad from his left paw. "Over my dead body, or should I say, over *their* dead bodies," Cat hissed.

Secret Agent
RAIF SINCLAIR
(SUPER SECRET AGENT)

Anthony Marchionda, Jr.

"Kill them. Kill them, both," Professor Vile ordered, in his thick Mandarin accent.

As Professor Vile's yacht swayed from side to side, Secret Agent Raif Sinclair realized that the XK-127 Pulse Blaster was of no use to him at that moment, being that it was locked in the trunk of his car.

"NO, WAIT," Sinclair cried out, as he tugged on the thick hemp ropes that tied him and the voluptuous, raven haired, French spy, Dominique Rochelle, to their chairs. "I'll make you a deal. I will hand over to you, the latest, secret technology that my country has to offer. All you have to do is let us go."

"What do you take me for, Mr. Sinclair? A fool?" Professor Vile asked.

"No, I'm serious. It's in the trunk of my car. Take us back to shore and it's yours."

"I would much more enjoy seeing you and your lady friend die a slow and agonizing death."

Sinclair thought for a moment. "Do what you want to the girl, just let me go and the weapon is yours."

"You bastard," Dominique exclaimed, her hot French blood boiling over. "I'll kill you myself."

"Come now, Mr. Sinclair. Do you expect me to believe that you, a top secret agent, would trade this beautiful young woman's life just to save your own?"

"Hay, I hardly even know her," Sinclair said, cavalierly.

"We're engaged to be married, you two-faced, lying bastard," Dominique fumed.

"I didn't really mean it."

"What do you mean, you didn't mean it?"

"It was just something I said in the heat of the moment."

"Just something you said?"

"Yes. It slipped out."

"Asking me to marry you, just slipped out?"

"You say things you don't mean, in those situations."

"Things you don't *mean*?…In those *situations*?"

"Yes."

"So, you only asked me to marry you so I'd have sex with you?"

"Well, I wouldn't put it that way."

"Then what way *would* you put it?"

"I don't know, I guess…"

"That's enough!" Professor Vile shouted. "Take her to my stateroom. I'll deal with her later."

"I'll get you Sinclair," Dominique shouted, as the henchmen picked her up, chair and all, and carried her off. "Somehow, some way, I'll get you for this."

"As for you Mr. Sinclair, I'm curious. Let us have a look at this new weapon of yours. If after I see it, I'm still not pleased, I can always allow the girl to kill you. That would be most amusing," he said as he began to chuckle. "Untie him."

The remaining henchmen quickly approached Sinclair and removed the ropes.

120

The moonless night sky made it difficult to tell where the ink black water ended and the pitch black night sky began. Professor Vile's yacht receded into the darkness as the speedboat raced towards the shore. As the speedboat reached the shoreline, the boat was throttled back. The henchmen jumped from the boat and secured it on the beach.

"Now, Mr. Sinclair, if you would be so kind as to lead us to your car. My patience is nearing an end."

"Right this way. Professor," Sinclair said, jumping from the speedboat.

As the henchmen and Professor Vile raced after Sinclair, he made his way up the beach and into the thick vegetation where he had concealed his car.

"Here it is, Professor," he said, making his way to the trunk of the Jaguar.

Professor Vile and his henchmen gathered around the trunk of Sinclair's car. Sinclair put the key in the lock and popped the trunk open. Inside was a small metal object no bigger than a cigarette lighter. Professor Vile reached in and picked up the object.

"This is your country's latest secret weapon? A cigarette lighter?" Professor Vile began to roll with laughter.

"I wouldn't laugh, if I were you. It's more than just a lighter," Sinclair said, as he turned the bezel on his wristwatch to three o'clock and then pressed the winding stem. He quickly jumped into the trunk and closed the lid. The XK-127 began to glow. In an instant, a searing flash of light engulfed Professor Vile and his henchmen, vaporizing them where they stood. After a few moments,

Sinclair slowly opened the trunk lid and peered out.

"I'll have to ask the boys in R and D about reducing the radius from ten feet to five feet," he said to himself.

Sinclair climbed out of the trunk. He saw the XK-127 lying on the ground and reached down to pick it up. Sinclair then took his cigarette case from inside his breast pocket and took out a cigarette. He flipped open the XK-127 and lit his cigarette. As he took a puff he looked out towards Professor Vile's yacht.

"I wonder how pissed off Dominique really is?" he said to himself. "Surely, my saving her life should be enough for her to forgive me?" He took another puff and stared out at the yacht.

"Knowing Dominique, I'd better stop by a jewelry store before rescuing her."

Sinclair dropped the cigarette to the ground, crushed it under his heel then straightened his white tuxedo jacket. He jumped into the Jaguar and sped off down the road, in search of the nearest jewelry store.

Lawrence Payne

"This is the section where I tell you about me."

"My name is Lawrence Payne. Ohio native. Computer geek. Author. And Buffy/Angel fanfic writer.

"I am not the type of person who is interested in the hagiography of the hero. I'm the kind of guy who loves to root for the bad guy. I love villains. Jason, Freddie Krueger, Michael Myers, the 'Scream' killers, the blood sucking vampire and the evil hellspawn, even Darth Vader and Emperor Palpatine are way more interesting than the so-called hero.

"When I watch a horror flick, I want the killer/monster to win. I tell the villain where the kids are hiding. 'He's hiding behind the tree! Behind The Tree! Get'em!' I hate it when they die at the end and it bugs me that at least one kid always gets away.

"My motto. If you've ever said, 'Hey! Let's go to a deserted cabin deep in the woods with no phone. Six kids were killed there last year. It'll be fun!' You deserve to be chopped into little pieces with a machete."

An Exercise in Power

Lawrence Payne

"Yeah but!" Matthew Woods frantically shouted.

Matthew stood with his hands raised in defiance in front of the mass of angry youngsters that made up his tenth grade class. His voice was hoarse as he yelled, raspy and sore, strained almost to the breaking point in a desperate attempt to be heard over the violent clamor.

"But nothing!" roared Carly Edwards, her fist pumping wildly in the air. Her 14-karat gold 'What Would Jesus Do' bracelet became a chorus of mini church bells, clanging and rattling to the rhythm, as it banged furiously against her tiny wrist. The starched white silk of her school uniform was slick with sweat, sticking to her armpits like a second skin.

"This is a place of sin!" she shouted back, her eyes ablaze with righteous fury. "It is an abomination against the Lord! It must be destroyed!!!"

"This isn't a 'place of sin' !" Matthew yelled, desperate to interject some reason into this insane situation. "It's a house Carly! A house!! It's someone's home! People live here!!"

"People who stand against the Lord. Heretics who defile the Word of God!"

"Teaching science isn't amoral, but what you're doing right now is!! Damn it Carly! STOP THIS!!!"

Matthew turned his attention to the crowd, "EVERYONE!! LISTEN TO ME!! PLEASE!! You can't destroy someone's home just because you disagree with what he teaches!"

"We can!! And by God, we will!!"

Carly turned to face the crowd of teenagers she had

marched here from the high school less than two hours ago. Like a general commanding her troops, she stared into the sea of pressed, white, cotton shirts and blue blazers, making eye contact with each of her minions. She raised her right hand majestically skyward. Her stance was that of a queen addressing her subjects. The light and strength of her father, the Prophet James Edwards, shone in her eyes as she commanded, "DESTROY THIS HOUSE OF SIN!!!"

Matthew watched in horror as 22 children from the Mary of Christ Middle School transformed into a violent mob. The light of virtue that had once shone brightly in their young eyes was gone, replaced by a blazing fire of hate. In unison, the children roared an unholy battle cry before charging the house.

Matthew's heart sank into his stomach as dozens of his friends and classmates stormed pass him screaming Carly's final words like irate drones. His mind was racing, transfixed by the terror before him, desperately trying to make some kind of sense of it all. His feet turned to clay, as he stood riveted in the spot were he made his final plea.

Rocks thrown in heated zeal became missiles that shattered windows and dented walls. Flowers were trampled, the life stomped out of them by angry young feet. Doors were shattered, hammered down by makeshift bats. Once the doors were gone, the mob forced their way inside.

Dozens of irate teens rampaged within the structure, kicking over furniture, smashing family heirlooms, pulling family photos out of lovingly framed cases before ripping them to shreds and destroying everything in their path.

Then came the fire.

Alcohol soaked rags were stuffed into gasoline filled bottles and ignited. The crude wicks burned quickly as the bottles were thrown. If this had been any other setting, the burning cocktails flying across the night sky would have been a beautiful sight. Instead, it was a nightmare of smoke, heat and burning wood.

The smoke turned the howling mob back into children when everyone started coughing. The children who were still inside the now intensely burning structure panicked as the flames quickly rose around them. The frightened children were grabbed and led out by the others.

Smoke filled Matthew's nostrils, causing him to cough. The minor irritation in his throat helped him regain his composure, pulling him back to the here and now. He turned away from the growing flames and ran down the street. Seeking escape from the heat and soot, the other children soon followed. Everyone gathered on the corner about a block away, and watched the McPherson's home burn from a safer distance.

After the violence, there was silence. Beyond the occasional cough and slight gag, no sounds could be heard.

"We should get going," Luke Benson said. "It's going to rain soon." His tone was that of someone who was unable to take the silence, so he tried to fill the empty space with sound. The silence gave him, gave everyone, too much time to think.

No one spoke a word.

"We did good. Right?" Jonnie Runmo quietly asked. Her mouth —still not use to the newly placed braces- formed small puddles of spit in the corners as she talked.

Again, no reply. The awful silence continued.

Matthew searched the crowd for Carly. He found her sitting on the curb. She was coughing up the small amount of smoke that had entered her lugs.

Matthew ran over to Carly. He grabbed her tightly by her arms while he pulled the girl to her feet.

"Why?!" he demanded as he locked his eyes on hers. "Why did you do this?!"

Carly said nothing. She just stood there, silent and expressionless, returning his gaze with empty eyes.

"WHY CARLY?!!" Matthew yelled while tightening his grip. This time he forcefully shook her.

A small smile formed on Carly's face.

Matthew tightened his grasp on Carly's arm even further. Even though she was clearly in pain, she did not try to break free. She just stood there, calmly smiling at him.

"SAY SOMETHING GODDAMN IT!!" The obscenity felt odd in his mouth, but he said it anyway. At this point, his ire had completely overwhelmed his sense of modesty.

Again, Carly gave no reaction. She was calm throughout his interrogation. She kept her eyes fixed on his, but she still did not utter a word. She knew her silence was a far more cutting blow then anything she could have said.

Carly finally broke her silence.

"I," she calmly explained, "Didn't do anything. McPherson brought this on himself."

"How? How did he bring this on himself?"

"He defied the Lord."

"By teaching a class you and your father don't agree with?"

" 'And God said, Let the earth bring forth the living creature after his kind, cattle, and creeping thing, and beast of the earth, after his kind: and it was so. And God said...' "

" '...Let us make man in our image,' " Matthew interrupted. " 'After our likeness: and let them have dominion over the fish and the fowl...' Don't quote the Bible to me Carly. I went to all of the same Bible Study classes you did."

"Then you know why."

"No. I don't."

"We are not monkeys, Matthew. We are the true children of God. And as such we have a right... No... A duty to punish those who commit blasphemy."

"Creationism isn't blasphemy," Matthew said as he launched into old form. He was still 'putting on his old debater's hat' as his mother would say. After everything he had seen this night, he still believed logic and reason would win the day.

"It's just another theory of how life started on Earth," he continued. "It's a belief system, just like ours, only it's different. Professor McPherson isn't defying God by teaching it. He isn't defying anyone..."

Matthew paused to contemplate his own words.

"...But you. That's what all of this was really about wasn't it? You... This wasn't about Professor McPherson teaching Evolution, or the school board saying he could. This was all about you."

Carly's silence and her calm smile returned.

Matthew let go of Carly. His hand flopped to his sides. A look of pure puzzlement came over his face.

"Why?" he asked again. This time, all of the anger was gone from his voice.

Carly cupped her hand to the side of her mouth. She leaned forward, balancing on her toes to match his added height, and gestured for Matthew to bend down. In a calm factual tone, she whispered in his ear, "Because I can."

The words hit Matthew like a freight train. The full realization of the day's events suddenly became crystal clear. She meant that. More than anything else she had said on this dreadful day, Matthew realized that those three words were the most truthful things Carly had said all night. This was nothing more than an exercise in power. Every insane act of cruelty he had witnessed since this evening began had been done on a whim, all to amuse a spoiled child.

"The debate," he whispered, "was a sham. Every word you said, every point you made, every fact you disputed, all of it was a lie. You didn't mean a word of it. Professor McPherson meant nothing to you. You just used him to get everyone angry."

Matthew paused before he said, "Angry enough to do this. You destroyed a man's home just because you had the power to."

Mixed with Matthew's newfound revelations was a fair amount of fear. He stepped away from her. Carly's smile was now wide and strong. His eyes stayed fixed on hers, unsure of exactly what would happen if he dared turn them away.

There was another seemingly endless silence as the two youngsters faced off, both silently expecting the other to make the first move. The sound of sirens in the distance broke the tension.

Carly was the first to act. She calmly turned away from Matthew.

The other children quickly cleared a path for her as she began to walk home. The rest soon followed suit. Everyone scattered and ran for their respective homes.

Matthew did not leave. He turned back to stare at the ever-growing flames.

His time was limited and he knew it. The sirens grew closer with every passing second. If he didn't leave now, he was sure to get caught, and getting caught meant answering a lot of questions. Part of him wondered if that was such a bad thing.

On the one hand, Matthew knew he was one of the few people in town who knew the whole story. When Professor McPherson got approval from the school board to teach a class on Evolution, he had inadvertently tapped into a deep vein of anger that ran throughout the township. A war of ideologies soon followed. A war that, before tonight, remained fairly civil. Carly used that anger to her own means. But this was beyond a simple disagreement. This was an out-right crime.

Someone had to expose Carly for the monster she was.

On the other, Matthew realized this had the potential to blow up in his face. Carly had done some bad things in the past, but she had never done anything like this before. Could he just sit back and let her get away with something this terrible?

Would anyone even believe him? All of the other kids heard Carly's admission, but he knew none of his classmates would ever admit their crimes. And even if she did get caught, would she get into any real trouble, or would her father just use his influence to get her out of it?

Carly's father was the most prominent and powerful citizen in Auburndale County. Going up against her meant going up against the entire Edwards clan, and no one was about to do that. Besides, if he turned her in, he risked becoming a pariah. These were just some of the questions that ran through his mind.

The sirens were much closer now. The flashing red and white lights of the fire-truck could now be seen moving towards him.

Moment of truth.

Be here when the cops arrive or take off like everyone else? Matthew only had a few seconds to decide.

Matthew took one last look at the burning husk that was once the McPherson family home.

A single tear ran down his cheek as he said, "I'm

sorry."

Matthew turned and ran for home.

A Drink From The Well of Inspiration

Lawrence Payne

" 'It was a cold winter morning in Moscow. The air carried a certain... certain... Je ne se quoi?' "

"No," said Edward Morse as he sat at his desk. "That's not right."

The crisp, white sheet of paper was quickly pulled from the antique Granville Automatic typewriter. He crumpled the paper in his hand before chucking it into the nearby wastebasket. A fresh blank sheet was gently inserted.

Edward stretched his body, elongating his tall slender frame by encircling his fingers behind his back and aching forward. Small dustings of gray were peppered throughout his hair and body, there presence just beginning to show in the sea of matted and tangled brown.

"Okay," Edward said as he exhaled from his stretch. He cracked his knuckles and wiggled his fingers. "From the top."

" 'It was a cold winter morning in Moscow. The air was thick with... anticipation.' "

"Anticipation? How can the air have 'anticipation'? Only people can have that." Edward massaged his eyes with his thumb and index finger before quickly crumpling, discarding and replacing the offending passage.

"It was a dark and stormy..."

"NO!! NO!! NO!!!"

A deep exhale followed by a gentle massage of his temple preceded yet another exchange of paper.

"Okay. Forget the Moscow bit, focus on our hero."

" 'Kirk awoke to a myriad of pleasant sensations. A warm brush of air against his face, the smell of freshly cut roses, the touch of satin sheets against his skin and the unmistakable feel of a warm female body pressed tightly against his own.' "

"Arggh!! What am I thinking! I can't use that again. That's how I started my last book."

Another paper crumpled and discarded; another fresh piece inserted; another opening passage was written; and yet another paper was quickly discarded. This pattern continued for eight hours straight. The small white wastebasket next to his desk, having reached capacity long ago, now overflowed with wads of discarded paper.

" 'Kirk walked down the streets of Moscow with a purpose. He had to deliver the roll of microfilm he had just procured from his fellow British spies in the Russian Consulate to his sexy contact, Tasha, before the KGB discovered his presence and jailed him as a spy.' "

"Ohh that's just great! Give up the whole plot in the first sentence. Brilliant writing there Bub!"

This time, Edward ripped the paper from the typewriter before violently smashing the offending passage in his hand and throwing it to the ground. Another clean sheet was rammed into the typewriter.

140

" 'It was love at first sight. The first time Kirk laid eyes on Tasha's long silky legs, tall fit frame and sensuous curves, he fell madly in love with her. Kirk was in the hospital with a pain in his liver that fell just short of being jaundice. The doctors were puzzled by the fact that it wasn't quite jaundice. If it had become jaundice, they could treat it. If it became jaundice and went away, they could discharge him. But this 'just being short of jaundice all the time' just confused them...' "

Edward stared at the words for several long minutes. His temple throbbed with pain as he read the passage over and over again. A powerful anger grew in his mind while waves of nausea flooded his body.

"Damn it! Damn It! DAMN IT!!" he screamed at the top of his lungs. "No one's going to notice that you just plagiarized Heller's greatest work, you stupid SON OF A...!!!"

Edward yanked the paper from the typewriter and ripped it to shreds in a fit of uncontrolled anger.

A series of 4 short thuds were heard coming from the far wall of his apartment. His neighbor, Old Lady Ferguson, was banging her cane on the wall they shared. It was her not so subtle way of reminding him to keep the noise down.

Edward responded to her request in his usual manner. He banged the flat side of his fist against the wall as he boisterously shouted a string of obscenities at her. As usual, Misses Ferguson chose to end the conversation right then and there.

With his neighborly distractions now concluded, Edward returned his attention to his work. Defeated, he collapsed on top of his typewriter in tears.

"I'm a hack!" he cried, saying the words over and over as he banged his head against the Granville.

He lifted his head from the typewriter and stared at the ceiling.

"I'm a has been!" he screamed, "A nobody! My tombstone will read, 'Here lies Edward Morse. He wrote a really good book a few years ago. Now, he's a worthless hack! He died... whenever, but he was dead to the world at age 34!' "

Edward flopped his head forward. He stared at the photos of H. P. Lovecraft, Robert E. Howard and Robert Heinlein that hung on the wall above his desk. Each one had been lovingly placed in a solid gold frame years ago; they were one of the few things he had bought with his newfound literary success.

"How did you do it!?" He asked the photos. "How did you keep the ideas flowing? How do you write great story after great story for years on end? How!?"

He stared at the pictures intently, locking eyes with the eyes of each of the photos. His conscious mind knew that they could not respond to his request, but he still demanded answers.

"USELESS HACKS!!" he yelled at the pictures. He picked up one of the discarded paper wads and forcefully threw it at the center photo. The paper bounced off the picture frame and landed near his feet without any damage being done.

He stared at his typewriter next. The antique Granville Automatic was yet another purchase made possible by his literary success. He had paid a ridiculous

142

amount of money for the aged antique at a high-end auction house in New York.

The Granville's functionality was clearly not what made it expensive. Any brand of modern day computer would have done a much better job of putting his text onto paper than this antique. What made the Granville special, and expensive, was its previous owner.

This was the exact same typewriter that Robert E. Howard had used to create his stories. Every day Howard would sit at this very machine and craft the fantastic tales that he would sell to Weird Tales Magazine. This was also the same machine that Howard had used to write his greatest masterpiece, the collective works of Conan and the Hyborian Age. Those were the greatest set of books and short stories Edward had ever read. They literally changed his life. They fired his imagination and stirred his soul. It was those books that made him want to become a writer.

But that was then. Those books did nothing now to rekindle his passion. He silently wondered if anything ever could.

Edward flopped back down into his chair in defeat. He folded his arms on the desk and rested his head on them.

A few minutes later, he drifted off into a fitful sleep.

* * * *

Edward was awakened from his labored rest by the feel of a soft hand gently caressing his face. He awoke to find a woman standing next to his desk.

To call her beautiful would be a horrible misuse of the word. She was stunning. Beyond stunning. She was breathtaking. Awe-inspiring. Overwhelmingly beautiful! None of the pathetic descriptions his puny mind could come up with could truly do her justice.

She radiated youth and beauty. Trails of twinkling light flowed behind her, sparkling like rivers of diamonds in the sunlight. Her face was bathed in a golden glow that emanated from her soul. Her skin shined with passion and vigor. Her incredibly long, golden brown hair, a shock or storm of hair, fluid and free, waved as it streamed behind her, glistening as it flowed pass her shoulders. Every strand moved in unison as if they were guided by an unfelt wind.

She wore a long green and gold dress that shimmered like rays of sunshine as it flowed against her thin, fit frame. The dress moved in rhythm with her hair, the mysterious wind guiding them both.

Adding to her already unbelievable beauty was the fact that she was almost translucent. As she stood next to his desk, she floated several inches off of the ground; her unseen feet never touched the hardwood floor of his midtown apartment.

"Who are you?" Edward asked as he stared at the woman in disbelief.

"I am a muse." The woman answered. Her voice was gentle and soft, like the rousing harmony of a choir of angels.

"How did you...?"

"You called out to me."

"Called out to you?"

"With your pain."

She gestured at the photos. "All of them have called to me at various times in their lives. Each one seeking the same thing. Inspiration. They were willing to give. And I have always provided."

"You can give me inspiration!?" Edward said. The excitement in his voice was unmistakable.

"Yes. If you can meet my payment."

"Payment?"

"A part of your soul."

Edward considered her word for a whole 30 seconds before he shouted, "Yes! YES!! I'll do it! Whatever it takes!"

The Muse reached out a delicate hand, and rested it gently on his forehead. Her skin was smooth, soft to the touch. Her hand glowed brighter as it touched him, filling his mind with words, images and new thoughts.

*   *   *   *

Edward awoke from his desk with a start. He jerked his head so far forward he bumped it against a nearby lamp. A string of obscenities erupted from his mouth as he rubbed the pain from his forehead.

Once again Old Lady Ferguson banged her cane against the wall.

"Put a sock in it!" Edward yelled back. He punctuated his order with a couple of loud slaps against the wall.

When the pain and the neighborly interruption subsided, an odd sense of calm came over him. The room fell silent.

For several minutes, stillness gripped the air. Edward stared at the antique Granville. He was relaxed and patience, calmly waiting for some unknown event to happen. Suddenly, the silence of the room was shattered by the sound of busy fingers banging furiously on small steel keys. A torrent of words and images, descriptions, phrases, metaphors and similes roared into his consciousness. Furious digits banged feverishly on tiny metal keys. His hands could barely keep up with the words that flowed from his mind. The flood almost overwhelmed him, threatening to consume his psyche if he did not release them.

* * * *

" '...The passion between them could no longer be denied. Tasha kissed Kirk with all of the hunger that burned inside her. Their kiss ended, she stared deeply into his eyes.

'Will we ever be free, Kirk?' she asked. 'Will we be free of this life of danger and intrigue?'

'As long as the nations of this world are constantly seeking to destroy each other,' Kirk said. 'I'll be there. As long as injustice reigns, I'll be there. To stop it.'

Tasha pressed her body tightly against his. Kirk returned her embrace as he looked out over the French Rivera. He could rest for a time, but not for long. The world was safe once again, but only for now.

Kirk knew that his talents would soon be needed.

Just not right now. Now, he was going to find love and comfort in Tasha's warm embrace.

The End.' "

Edward pulled the final sheet of paper from Granville and gently placed it face down on top of the large stack that sat next to his typewriter. He leaned back in his chair. A broad smile formed on his face as he stretched his neck and interlaced his fingers behind his head. A final exhausted breath escaped his body as he realized the incredible truth.

He did it.

He finished his second novel.

And it felt wonderful.

A sense of calm and inner peace came over him. For the first time in a long time, Edward was truly at ease.

For Edward Morse there was no greater feeling in the world than putting a novel to bed. He tried to remember the last time he felt this relaxed. The day he finished his first book was the only thing that came to mind. He tried to recall other happy memories, but nothing came close to the emotional high he was on right now. His first date with his childhood sweetheart, his first kiss, taking his childhood sweetheart to the high school prom, going to his first real college party, the day he met the woman who would be his wife, his wedding, his honeymoon in Vegas, the day he signed the divorce papers and ended his two year marriage to the neurotic tramp he now happily refers to as his ex-wife, even the day the Sox won the World Series, everything paled in comparison to the joy he felt right now. At this moment, all was right with the world.

The phone rang.

"Hello!" An unusually happy Edward beamed into the phone.

"Morse?! Damn it, man! Where the hell have you been?" The gruff voice on the other end was that of Carl Runmo, Edward's publisher and long time friend.

"Carl!!" Edward cheerfully replied. "I got it, buddy!"

"Got what?"

"My second novel."

"Forget about that! Where the hell have you been!?"

"What do you mean 'where have I been?' I've been here, writing this new book. You're going to love it, Carl! It's got everything. Exotic locations, incredible beauties, tons of action and intrigue and surprises! It's fantastic."

"Don't you answer your damn phone anymore? I've been trying to contact you, but no one's heard from you in the last month or so."

"Month?" Edward asked.

"Yes, you idiot! The last month or so! You missed three scheduled appearances, and all of your book signings.

"Two weeks ago, the BookTV television network called me. They wanted you to be on a panel of authors to discuss the state of modern literature. They called me because they haven't been able to contact you. Hell, no one has been able to contact you! I've been getting calls from your friends and family members, all of whom keep asking me if I've seen or heard from you lately. And, no one has been able to get inside your apartment. Your door is sealed shut and apparently your landlord has pulled a disappearing act too. It's like you dropped off the face of the Earth!"

Edward dropped the phone. He could still hear Carl screaming something or other on the other end, when he decided to check himself out.

Edward looked down at his stomach. His already thin malnourished form now showed signs of serious deterioration. His formerly flat stomach was distended and swollen with hunger. His arms and legs were bony, weakened to the point of breaking from weeks of atrophy. He felt his face. He could feel the hollowed out cheekbones and sunken skin. He looked at his hands. They were the only part of his body that was not thin from starvation. His fingers were puffy and bloated, the skin on the tips had been worn down so severely he could see the lines and definitions of bone. Some of his fingers were actually bleeding, the skin completely worn away by endless hours of use.

Edward looked out of his window. A brisk wind was blowing through the city streets. The leaves on the sidewalk trees had just begun to change color, a far cry from the balmy heat he had experienced the last time he was outside.

On wobbly knees, Edward walked to the small mail slot on his front door. It was overflowing with unopened mail. Intermixed with the usual junk mail was a heap of unpaid bills along with dozens of letters from concerned friends and family, all strewn in a small pile on the floor.

A quick glance at his answering machine completed the story. The small white box continually flashed the number 46 at him, while the 'replace tape' light constantly blinked red.

Edward recalled the Muse's final words. *"The payment,"* he thought. *"She demanded a part of my soul, but she did not say how it would be done. This must have been it."*

The reality finally hit him. The muse had given him the inspiration he needed, but she had stolen a part of his life in return. He had completely lost the last 30 days. He needed some time to contemplate the meaning of it all.

Edward remembered a biography of Robert E. Howard he had read years ago. In it, the author said that Howard was prone to fits depression and intense anger. To cure these bouts of fear and anxiety, he would lock himself in his room. It also said that Howard would have incredibly long marathon writing sessions. He would spend days, even weeks, locked away with his typewriter, pounding away at the keys with the fury of a madman. Edward had never understood that part of his literary hero's life, until now. Howard must have had several visits from a certain translucent, and now mutual, friend.

Edward stared at his hands and body a second time, again quietly contemplating the cost. Then he looked over at the large stack of papers on his desk. Over 600 neatly typed, single-spaced pages, each one a landmark of literary genius. With a little padding and an extraneous character or two thrown in, there was enough there to turn this one story into a three or four part book series.

"Totally worth it," he said to himself as he turned his attention back to the stack of papers. He had drunk from the well of inspiration. And even now, after finishing an entire novel, he was hungry for another taste.

"Thank you Muse," he said as he looked up, a large smile on his face.

"I hope we meet again soon."

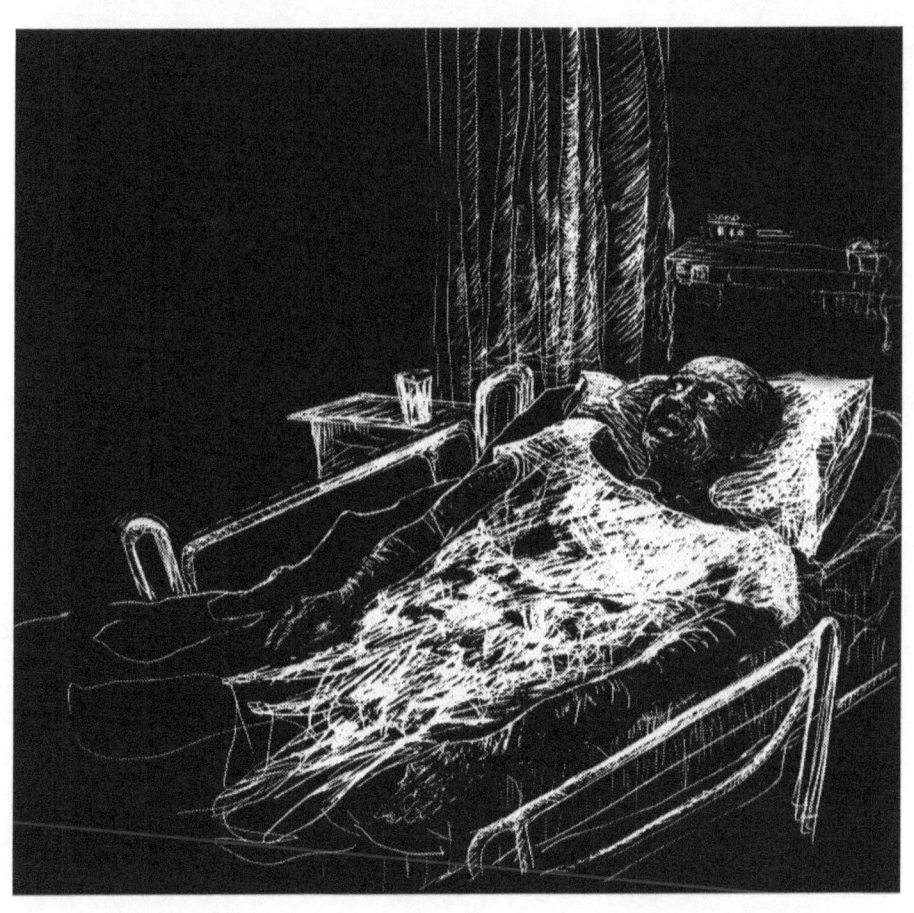

"The Night Weights Heavy..."

Lawrence Payne

Charles Jackson sat restlessly in his hospital bed. He stared at the blinking lights on the medical equipment as they rhythmically danced across the screen. The pain from the stab wound in his stomach was gone, but the pain in his heart was as sharp as ever. The high-pitched sound of the heart monitor beeped in a steady cadence, creating a constant and balanced rhythm that matched the dancing glow of the green lights.

Charles hated that sound. It was a constant reminder of his continuing life. The smell of powder and antiseptic mixed with a light scent of pine was yet another loathed constant of his hospital stay. The unvarying cleanliness was a prison in and of itself. Charles was stuck, confined to a germ-free cell of perfect sanitation. A place that had been scrubbed free of life, a sterile and bland world within which nothing new could grow for fear of being labeled unclean and suddenly scrubbed away. It was an oddly fitting penalty for someone who had committed his crimes.

As he shifted in his bed, he stared at the IV in his arm. He wondered why it was there. Why was he still here? Why was he still alive? And why did she have to...

Charles stopped staring at his IV and leaned back. He knew his bed was pressed up against the wall, but he did not care. He let his neck go limp while he fell backward into the mattress, intentionally banging the back of his head against the hard concrete wall. The pain gave him an odd kind of comfort.

As he lay in his hospital bed, his eyes now focused on the ceiling, he recalled the events of the last few months. He had no problem remembering the factual events; the details were easy and clear. In fact, he spent

155

most of his waking hours reliving them. The problem was his inability to make some kind of sense of it all. As real as he knew it was, it still felt like someone else's bizarre dream.

Then it happened.

Again.

"My, My! MY!! How the mighty have fallen?" A female voice taunted. As usual, it came from the darkest corner of the room. These little visits were yet another hated routine of his hospital stay. It was odd that she came around now. She never visited him before. Before everyone hated him. Before the man he thought was his friend tried to kill him. Before he got her...

"Go away," Charles said, his tone more of a plea than a command.

"Why should I? You never left me alone. You used me to justify everything you have ever done. Even this."

"That is not true."

"Isn't it? I am the reason you started hanging out with thugs. I am the reason you sold your soul to a bunch of drug dealers. The first time. I am the reason you ditched Duke and your old gang and ran with Knox. And I am the reason you decided to do what did. Everything in your life has evolved from those three things. But that's not important right now. The real question is why. Why did you do it? Was it really all for me, or was it all for love of money?"

Charles said nothing.

"Come on Charley!" the mystery voice taunted, "You're Mr. Big Shot Law Enforcer Man now. Your

Officer Ryan's goto guy. You're 'Working for The Man every night and day' as the old song goes. You have to say something."

"So what?"

"So what? So What!? You turn into a snitch and give up your boys to the cops for a few extra dollars in your pocket and a 'get-out-of-jail-free-card' and that's the best comeback you've got. 'So what'!?"

"So what if you're right?" Charles blasted back. "Yeah, my entire life has been about money. I ain't never had none. So I did what I had to do to get by. And OK... Maybe it wasn't all about you. Maybe it was about me. I had a seed to feed and wife to care for. That was all I cared about. I made some serious duckets in the game, enough for you, me and Lil' Nat to get the hell out of the Brier Hill Projects forever. Things was going great. Until..."

"Until now. What happened this time?"

Again Charles did not respond. He just continued to stare at the ceiling.

"Wooo! Stunned into silence again. Am I batting a thousand today or what!?"

His mysterious guest finally showed herself when she emerged from the darkened corner and stood in the light. His visitor was Alayna Jackson, Charles' dead wife.

Charles stared at his former wife. She looked exactly the same as she did the day he found her body. She was hollow. Her smooth, dark skin was pale and dry. She had two large puncture wounds in her chest, each stained with large tracks of blood that were sprayed across her t-shirt and jeans. Her eyes, which were once vibrant pools of life, were open and empty. Those same eyes now stared straight into his soul.

The sight of her triggered his memory. The day the two most beautifully bright lights in his dark and gloomy world were ended. Memories of the day Knox, the man he thought was his friend, took her life and the life of his eight-year-old son as retribution for his betrayal. It was a punishment they did not deserve, but because of his greed, it was one they had to endure.

For what? What offense was so horrible that his family had to suffer a greater punishment than him? Telling the cops where and when Knox got his drug shipments from? For wearing a wire and testifying against his former gang? For betraying the code of the streets? That was a joke. Since the day he was born, the street had done nothing but betray him. The streets had taken away all of his hopes and dreams, and left him with nothing but an empty hatred of life. He did not owe them, or the streets, any allegiance. All he owed, he had already paid in pain and suffering. Now the streets wanted blood, and thanks to his mistakes, they got that too.

Charles sat up in his bed again. He stared at his hands as they rested in his lap.

"Don't go blaming them," Alayna scolded. "It's not their fault."

"I know," Charles said.

"Then whose fault is it?"

"It was Knox. He did this."

"Wrong again big bro. Try Another!"

Try Another was a game he and Alayna use to play as kids. It was a lot like 20 Questions only with people. One of them would think of someone who lived in the neighborhood, and the other would try to figure out who it was. It was one of the few truly happy memories from his childhood. When Charles saw his son playing it with his friends, it always made him smile. Now, it caused him nothing but pain.

"Knox!..." Charles began. He was finally breaking out of 'zombie mode'. His voice showed real emotion for the first time.

"...Did exactly what he said he would do." Alayna interjected, cutting off his usual delusory rant. "It's what he was always going to do. He was planning this for years, bro. Years! He had to be. All those years he spent cooling his ass up at Rikers, he has had nothing but time to plan this. All he needed was the right time, the right person, and you in the right place."

Once again, there was nothing but silence from Charles. His eyes stayed fixed on his hands.

Alayna moved from the corner. She sat on the edge of his bed and looked her husband in the eyes.

" 'If you don't stand for something, you'll fall for anything' ", she said. "Isn't that what your momma use to tell you? 'You have got to keep your head screwed on straight.' Well. Did you listen? Have you kept your head screwed on straight? Have you Charley!? Naaa. You haven't. You let a bunch of drug-smokin punks mess with your head. Why? Because the 'legit life' wasn't moving fast enough for you. Because you thought you were too stupid to make it in the real world without taking the cheap shot?

You're not stupid baby. Let me rephrase that. You weren't stupid before, but you are now. Now, you are just stupid enough.

"Just stupid enough to abandon everything your Momma ever taught you. Just stupid enough to trust that fool Knox. Just stupid enough to let him talk you into selling his drugs for him, something you knew was wrong. Just stupid enough to rat out your partners to the police the first time you get into real trouble. Just stupid enough to let Knox and his gang find out that you were the one who sold them out. Just stupid enough to get the only two people in this world who ever loved you killed. And you are just stupid enough to help Knox kill..."

At that moment, Alayna face, body, and voice transformed into the dark skinned grinning visage of his former friend.

"Me!" Knox said in an ominous tone.

*　　*　　*　　*

Charles awoke from his nightmare in a cold sweat. He quickly sat up in his bed. He could feel his heart pounding in his ears. He was out of breath, his lungs burned from lack of oxygen. As he struggled to catch his breath, he searched the room for his wife. She was nowhere in sight.

The hospital intercom clicked on. The voice of one of the on-call nurses asked, "Are you alright Mr. Jackson?"

"What?"

"Are you alright? Your heart rate is at a very high level."

Charles wiped the sweat off of his face with his hand.

"Fine... I'm... I'm fine."

"Would you like a sedative to help you sleep?"

"No," Charles solemnly replied. "I've slept enough for one... for one lifetime."

Practice Time

Lawrence Payne

"Gently, Thomas," Mrs. Calas instructed as she swayed her arms to the rhythm. Her voice and tone were the soft coo of a Morning Dove, gently urging her pupil to fly to greater heights. "Gently. Let the music flow from your fingers like a warm summer rain."

Her long gray hair was pulled into a tight bun that sat on the middle of her head. As she talked, she waltzed gingerly across the hardwood floor, careful not to knock over any of the expensive furnishings and vases that lined the piano room.

Young Thomas Abrams tried his best to follow his teacher's instructions. He adjusted his stance, relaxed his fingers and cleared his mind again, but, as usual, it did little good. The sound that came out of the brown Yamaha Upright Piano as he played could not be called music. It was little more than noise.

"Slowly, Thomas," Mrs. Calas said. "Take it slowly. Relax. Feel the notes in your hands, let them flow from your fingers and into the piano."

Thomas relaxed his hands a second time and tried to let the music flow, but once again nothing but noise flowed from his fingers.

"It's hopeless!" Thomas exclaimed. In a fit of childish rage, he slammed his hands flat on the keyboard. "I can't do this!!"

"Yes you can," she said stopping her waltz midway and focusing her attention on him again. "You just need to relax. Concentrate. Focus your mind. Feel the music flow from within you."

"It's too hard."

"Stop trying so much. Just relax and feel. The music will come if you let it."

"But I don't feel anything when I play."

"And that is your problem. You're blocking. Let yourself feel the music within you."

"Maybe there is no music inside me!" Thomas screamed as he hammered his fist on the piano. His desire to master the piano was gone. At that moment, the tall brown box had become nothing more than a towering instrument of personal torture. All he had left was anger, and it had reached its peak. Anger at the piano itself, and everything associated with it, including Mrs. Calas.

Mrs. Calas did not react to his tantrum. She just stood there, silently staring at the young boy. After a few seconds of silent contemplation, she put her hand on her chest as a burst of uncontrolled laughter erupted from her lips. Her 70-year-old heart was not used to the strain.

Mrs. Calas knew the problem. She had always known. Young Master Thomas, at the tender age of six, was already starting to feel the weight of his legacy. All he had ever heard about, all anyone in his family had ever talked about, was how great a musician he was going to be.

Young Master Thomas had an impressive pedigree, to say the least. He was more than just the first-born son of a wealthy English family, he was the offspring and heir-apparent of two of classical music's most famous and successful figures.

His father, the great Thomas Abrams the Second, was a world famous musician and composer. A stalwart, self-made man who had taught himself to read and play music by the time he was 20, Thomas the Second, or Thomas Senior as he was now titled, was the most famous living composer of classical music in his time. For over 20 years, he had delighted audiences with his magnificent operas and original scores. The accolades from his immense body of work spanned several hallways of the Abram's manor.

Then there was his mother, the world-renowned opera singer and fellow composer Deborah Abrams. Deborah was well noted as a child prodigy in her native land of Ireland. She had penned two waltzes, a sonnets and a full musical score, all before the age of twelve. At 24, she was topping the bill at the London Palladium, wowing sold out crowds with her powerful vocals. At 30, she had brought the house down at London's famous Buxom Opera House with her moving rendition of Petra in The Bitter Tears of Petra von Kant. Her successes continued until she met, fell in love with, married, and bore the child of Thomas Senior. She announced her retirement to a stunned world two days before young Thomas was to be born.

On the day she and her husband introduced her newborn son to the Society pages, Deborah proudly proclaimed Young Master Thomas The Third would be the next great musician and composer of his time.

"You dear lad," Mrs. Calas said through the laughter. "I've known that for years."

Mrs. Calas got her laughter under control and sat next to the youngster on the piano stool.

"The day I met you was the day your parents hired me to teach you the piano. I told them, 'A child need time to learn complexities and intricacies of an instrument like the piano. Time,' I told them. 'Time and care. Don't rush the lad.' They did not listen. They assumed greatness from you. They had visions of you mastering instruments and penning great work while still in the womb. 'The minute my son sits in front of a piano, he will shine,' your father said. Your mother was a bit more realistic, but her expectations were still too high. She believed you would be playing the classics in perfect pitch and tone within a day. Not once did either of them consider the weight they were placing on your tiny, young shoulders."

Mrs. Calas held his face gently in her hands as she locked eyes with him.

"Stop it," she declared. "Stop worrying about your legacy and your heritage. Stop worrying. And just play."

With that, she kissed him on his nose and left the room. Once she was on the opposite side of the door, she put her hand to her ear and listened intently.

Thomas sat in his piano chair for a few moments as he contemplated his teacher's words. Was she right? Was he fighting his own skill? His young mind was not capable of understanding such complex judgments, but that did not stop them from dominating his thoughts.

After a few minutes, Thomas turned back to the piano. He gently placed his fingers on the keys, making sure to place them in their proper positions with a well-practiced ease.

Thomas began to play.

At that moment, something remarkable happened. Everything finally came into focus. Suddenly, it all made sense. Notes, rhythms, scale and pitch ceased to be abstract ideas and became real to him. All four converged in his mind to create a sound that did not irritate his ears. For the first time in his short life, Young Master Thomas Abrams was able to make music.

Thomas smiled. The joy on his face was unmistakable. He giggled gleefully as note after note ran from his hands and into the piano, creating a joyful opus of harmonious melodies. His instrument of personal torture had become a thing of pure joy.

"I'm doing it!" Thomas shouted as he increased the tempo. "I'm really doing it!!"

On the other side of the door, Mrs. Calas smiled widely.

"That's a good boy Thomas," she said as she renewed her waltz. "That's a very good boy indeed."

Diana Ludwig

The illustrator Diana Ludwig is a lazy bibliophile who helps to band ravens, map caves, and renovate planetariums. She once circumnavigated Pennsylvania alone on a bicycle. She has created chocolates for 17 years. While dreaming of revisiting Labrador & Newfoundland, she divides her time between studios in Allegheny National Forest & Youngstown, Ohio.

www.dianaludwig.com

www.ingramcontent.com/pod-product-compliance
Lightning Source LLC
Chambersburg PA
CBHW020610250626
47154CB00004B/1452